THE SILENCE OF THE SIRENS

Adelaida Garcia Morales won the prestigious Herralde Prize for Fiction in Spain with this, her second novel. Her first, *El Sur*, was made into a film in 1983.

ADELAIDA GARCIA MORALES

THE SILENCE
OF
THE SIRENS

Translated from the Spanish
by
Concilia Hayter

Flamingo
Published by Fontana Paperbacks

First published in Spain under the title
El Silencio de las Sirenas
by Editorial Anagrama, Barcelona 1985
First published in Great Britain
by William Collins 1988

This Flamingo Edition first published
in 1989 by Fontana Paperbacks,
8 Grafton Street, London W1X 3LA

Flamingo is an imprint of
Fontana Paperbacks, part of
the Collins Publishing Group

Typeset in Perpetua by
Ace Filmsetting Ltd, Frome, Somerset
Printed and bound in Great Britain by
William Collins Sons and Co. Ltd, Glasgow

For Victor

*For God permits that which does not exist
to be intensely illuminated.*

FERNANDO PESSOA

I

Elsa took leave of me in a brief letter: 'Maria, I leave you these gifts, keep them if you want to. Shall we meet again? love' – and forgot to sign it.

On a small wooden table covered with an ochre velvet cloth she had laid out different objects: a postcard reproduction of Paolo Uccello's *Saint George and the Dragon*; a dried blue flower, which she said was called 'love-in-a-mist'; an old Chinese box containing a photograph of her and copies of all the letters she had written to Agustín Valdés; a letter she had received from him, a portrait of Goethe contemplating a woman's face in silhouette; a platinum ring set with diamonds; a book, *Elective Affinities*; a reproduction of a Goya lithograph showing a man leaning over a woman, her face half-hidden by a mask, and the words, 'No one knows himself' written underneath. She had also left me a notebook, her own, in which she had written of her love for Agustín Valdés. And finally, a letter for Agustín that she had not yet sealed.

When I set out for this village where I met Elsa, I came with the intention of leaving it if I could not bear the solitude that awaited me. For though I have travelled quite widely and visited a number of towns in Spain and abroad, I have never felt drawn to lonely, isolated places, which have always struck me as nothing more than names on a map. Nonetheless, when I left the wilds of la Venta behind and reached the region of the Alpujarras, I felt I was crossing a precise frontier and entering a strange world, turned in upon itself, enclosed in timeless tranquillity. A multitude of little villages were hidden amongst the silent mountains, indifferent to that other world that remained outside, distant and confused. The road wound up through the mountains; the village was some five thousand feet above sea level. As I ascended, the silence that whistled in my ears grew in intensity. When at last I caught sight of the valley of the Poqueira I was overwhelmed: it was the most beautiful landscape I had ever seen in my life. The little white villages seemed to sleep, clinging like lichens to the sides and the summit of an enormous mountain. The intense sunlight of this land and the solemnity of the landscape filled me with such elation that for a moment all my fears vanished.

I spent the first night in the inn and when I awoke the next day it was already midday, but a dawn-like silence surrounded me. I went out for a walk and felt that I was in a different place from the village where I had arrived the previous day. A luminous mist covered the irregular streets and concealed the mountains. An immense cloud arose from the depths of the ravine pushed by a gentle wind. On both sides of the road fragments of green and leafy fields could be seen through gaps in the mist. I returned to the village and wandered through labyrinthine white streets. The clouds rolled down them, gradually covering the village. Faces emerged from the thick mist, faces with hardened, wrinkled skin, like uncouth masks. They appeared framed in windows or doorways, or could be glimpsed wandering about the maze of streets in which, from the very beginning, I felt trapped. They were faces full of infantile curiosity and they returned my greetings with looks that combined fear and hope, warmth and resentment. They made me feel that I was invading the intimacy of a large, peaceful family. But with the passing of time, I realized that the first impression gained of these villages as you approach from far off, as they sleep in the folds of the mountains or perch on their summits, is misleading. Later, when to some extent you have been adopted, if only with that dubious acceptance accorded here to outsiders, you find that you are surrounded by a veritable clamour. Little by little you realize that this apparent quiet might be anything, but not peace. Violent passions pull the strings of these lives that, at first, seem so serene. Behind their reserved even sullen expressions, there always beats a hostile mistrust, the memory of an ancient hatred not yet forgotten; the impossible love that destroyed a life. . . . Gradually you discover in the shifting eyes of these villagers a cruel indifference, a contemptuous curiosity; and also the sorrow of many separations, the sorrow of a village that is dying. You start seeing sickness everywhere, sickness that is not cared for: for here there is no money for prolonging useless lives.

The house that had been allocated to me as schoolteacher was appalling: it was almost square and its walls were too flimsy to stand up to the cold, the snow, the wind and the rain of these mountains. I finished by renting another in the village. It was one of those strange Berber constructions on several levels, with a fireplace, thick stone walls and a terraced roof covered in clay.

Sometimes I have cursed this village, its silence and stillness. In spite of that, I do not think I could leave it now, for again and again these mountains take me unawares through their perfect silence. They seem to spring up from the very darkness of the earth. They rear up here, eternally free and totally meaningless, like a landscape from before the coming of man. On their terraced slopes can still be seen the traces of colossal human effort. But an effort gone to waste after only a few scant years of neglect. Several generations of young men have refused the harshness of this country and emigrated to the factories and suburbs of big cities. And in the place of their work have appeared vast expanses of land now arid and gone to waste.

One of my most pleasant occupations was going for long walks in the surrounding fields, along the road or through the streets of the village. From the beginning I was struck by the number of solitary old women walking around everywhere. They were strange beings who seemed to live on the very boundary between life and death. They were women born with the century, slow-moving and dressed in mourning, who went about their daily tasks with a routine that seemed to hide something else – for their looks, always intent on something that was invisible to me, did not seem in any way connected with the words or actions that accompanied them. Sometimes I saw them as geometrical beings, nearly vegetable, whose movements were as mechanical as those of bees in a hive. At other times I thought I saw in their faces something that might be the stubborn remains of another culture, something that I could never know save in its most trivial aspects. When I watched them feeding their chickens, caring for the rabbits, sweeping the doorways of their houses, I liked to think that these actions took on for them dimensions unknown to me, as though they wove a complicated network of impenetrable emotions.

I wanted to know what it was that they had created in their lives to fill up so much solitude. On one occasion I mentioned this to Elsa, but she only wanted to know what they had invented that allowed them to give up love so serenely. For they were women who had given up being women to become something else, free now from the obligations of their sex. They could live alone without seeming to miss their loved ones, either dead or far away. They existed for no one and only one shadow darkened their lives: sickness, not death. Though, as they said themselves, the very worst was the hospital, that corpse factory, where they knew full well one could die simply of horror.

All I succeeded in getting from many of these old women was a timid greeting murmured as our paths crossed, even though they had been staring at me unabashed from a long way off. To me they all seemed totally ritualized. But nonetheless each one had her own individual stamp. Of course none of them caught my attention as strongly as Matilde with her strange gift – I shall come to that later. Before meeting her I had already heard the rumours that circulated about her in the village; underground rumours made up more of silences and frightened looks than of words. But I think that what really aroused my curiosity was her relationship with Elsa, whom I first met in her house.

Matilde was a little old woman, thin and short,

and her eyes looked out unabashed and penetrating. One day I went up to her as she sat in the sun outside her front door. I greeted her and she answered smiling. So I stopped and said: 'What lovely weather!' for with these women, I don't know why, I can never think of anything better to say.

'Yes, it's a very clear day,' she answered, and pointed with a finger at the inverted triangle the sea formed on the horizon where two mountains met. 'Look,' she said, 'those are the mountains of Barbary.'

I fixed my eyes on the triangle of sea and saw some ghostly shadows like doubtful mountains. It was the coast of Africa.

'They sometimes appear like that, in the sea,' she explained eagerly.

The mountains of Barbary meant the country of the Moors. These villagers seemed to suspect that they still lingered on here, hidden in the cliffs, trying to recover the treasures they had buried under the snow or under the fields that their skill had first cultivated. They have already been back once, so some say, more ferocious than ever, in Franco's war, enlisted in his army. The memory of their savage attacks still remains.

But they did not succeed in getting back their lands nor in disinterring their treasures. The Alpujarras seemed to think of them as personal enemies. And when, in spring, the swallows are late in coming, there are people who say – I myself have heard them – that the Moors kill the swallows as they fly over Africa to stop them from ever reaching these mountains.

2

After living in the village for a month, my relationship with the inhabitants was exactly what it had been the day I arrived. Many of them still turned round when our paths crossed and stood in the middle of the street staring at me with an effrontery that I found intolerable. It was as though they thought I could not see them, or that my seeing them or what I thought of them had no importance. In the beginning I exchanged a few words with the old women who sat enjoying the midday sun, always the same words about the weather or the peace of the village and the turmoil of towns. Matilde too made more or less the same vague remarks as the others, but I had the feeling that she was studying me attentively from behind her words, which formed between us a veritable curtain that concealed her real self. However, even these slight contacts were halted by the cold of winter which made them shut themselves up in their houses.

One night, for the first time, someone

knocked at my door. It was a woman who told me her name was Maria, the same as mine. Matilde had sent her to fetch me. She seemed to be about sixty years old but her body had kept an extraordinary vitality and in her face, now deeply lined, could be seen the vestiges of considerable beauty. After introducing herself and informing me of the reason for her visit, she said, 'Have you ever heard speak of the evil eye?'

'Yes, of course. Who hasn't heard about such things?'

'Matilde can cure it,' she said, lowering her voice as though imparting a secret; and added immediately, 'Some people have a power of destruction in their look. It's said they have a horse in their eyes. Everything they look at they destroy. I don't really believe in it too much myself, but just in case, if a woman passes in front of my door and I have doubts as to whether she does or doesn't and she looks at my flower pots, what I do, secretly, quietly, just to myself, is to say "God bless you". And then she can't do it, because it's none of God's work, but rather the devil's, so if you say God's name it doesn't work. They cast it at plants and animals and people, especially children. But they do it mostly to goats when they're going to have young. That's why in the old days they used to put a coloured ribbon on the collar with the bell, to cool the fire of the evil eye. But nowadays, most people don't believe in that sort of thing, so nobody puts a ribbon on their she-goats anymore.'

At that time of night my favourite place was in front of the fire. But it was the first time that anyone in the village had invited me to their house, so I followed Maria more out of politeness than curiosity. The evil eye had never really aroused my interest and struck me as trivial and absurd. The ceremony of fumigation that she started describing to me sounded as boring as Mass. What really excited my curiosity was the idea of Matilde in the presiding role.

When we entered Matilde's house, the first thing I saw was the goat, standing motionless in a corner with the quiet dignity that only goats possess. Nobody paid any attention to it, even though it was the reason for the ceremony. On seeing me Matilde limited her greeting to her usual smile. She glided between the shadows of her kitchen with rapid, precise movements. She alone prepared everything that would be necessary to conjure the evil eye that afflicted the ani-

mal. In the meantime I was introduced to the
third Maria, for there had to be three of us. She
was somewhat younger than the one who had
come to fetch me, very thin, her hair gathered in
a bun at the nape of her neck. In her face, only
her enormous black eyes, profoundly sombre,
seemed alive. Suddenly three little men came in,
joking among themselves. They were the three
Juans, also essential for the fumigation. They
seemed ill at ease and all three looked rather
alike. They fidgeted in front of the fire and I
thought they looked like schoolboys trying to
act like sceptical young men, betrayed by their
nervous laughter, their timid voices and their
anxiety. . . . In contrast, the women were serene
and serious, aware of the importance of what
they were doing. They looked at the Juans with
maternal tolerance until, suddenly, the youngest
of the Marias lost patience and ordered them to
be quiet.

'That's enough,' she said firmly. 'This is no
laughing matter. We know what we're doing. All
we do is pray to the saint until the crisis is over.'

As she said these words, evidently intended for
the three Juans, she looked intently at me, who
meanwhile had been keeping as quiet as the goat.

I didn't dare make the slightest murmur of sound. I felt that my presence there, at that time, was, to say the least of it, an impertinence. I was sure the others were aware of it too. Matilde treated me like a stranger – though, in fact, her attitude was one of solemn aloofness towards all of us. When she finally gave the signal to begin she seemed to be a different woman. From a beam in the ceiling she had taken down a bunch of rosemary tied with twine. With a pair of tongs she put hot embers from the fire in an earthenware bowl. She herself placed us in a ring, alternating Juans and Marias. She went from one to another and rather than walking seemed to glide, weightless, coordinating her movements with harmony worthy of a ballet, whilst from each of us she cut a lock of hair and a piece of clothing. She placed them all in the same bowl along with the glowing embers. Finally she added incense and rosemary. That same silence of the mountains and of the night then entered the room. She had taken position with the goat and the smoking bowl in the centre of the ring; as the bowl passed from hand to hand she prayed: 'By the three persons of the Most Holy Trinity . . . take it you, Maria . . . take it you, Juan. . ..'

Watching Matilde wrapping the goat in her movements, enveloping the animal in smoke, I thought for the first time that the evil eye must be something: a mysterious gesture of the soul, an evil vibration let loose . . . a word laden with hatred. I did not know what explanation could be given to whatever it was that kept these villagers reverently united in a rite that only the goat and I did not seem to understand. But, confronted by this old woman, stiff and solemn, incensing the mysteriously sick animal, I felt a deep respect. In this role she seemed to be transformed, younger and slimmer. Her unblinking eyes, fixed on the udder of the goat, had become extraordinarily large. Two Juans had lifted the goat shoulder high. Finally Matilde put down the smoking bowl and filled a white cup with water. She dipped three fingers of her right hand in oil and allowed one drop to trickle down from each finger onto the surface of the liquid she held in her right hand. She had just traced a question in the water in the shape of the three points of a triangle. Surely she did not know what or whom she interrogated, but whatever it might be, it would answer in the same language: if the drops dissolved in the water, the evil eye would disappear.

But if, on the contrary, they remained intact, each in its place, the victim of the spell would die.

When everyone had left, I approached Matilde who was looking with satisfaction at the drops, already shapeless and dissolved in the water. She had succeeded in exorcizing the evil from which the goat suffered.

Turning to me, she said only: 'It's as cold as death!'

'Why was it me you sent for?' I asked without any preamble.

'Because your name is Maria.'

'But I thought these things were very secret.'

'Indeed they are. But you could come.'

I tried to question her, but, friendly and aloof, she showed extraordinary skill in giving airy replies to all my questions without really answering any of them. I left thinking that this woman was more civilized than I. She, at least, possessed complete control over each of her gestures, her facial expressions, the tone of her voice, her words.

3

Barely two weeks had elapsed since I had taken part in the fumigation ceremony, when, once again, the same Maria came to fetch me one night. This time she did not even ask me whether I wanted to accompany her. From the doorway, without even coming in, she called: 'Hurry up! They're waiting for us.'

'For Heaven's sake,' I protested, annoyed. 'Do they cast the evil eye here every other day? It must be quite a job!' She answered, visibly offended, that this time it hadn't been cast in this village.

I was taken aback and feared that Matilde was charged with exorcizing the evil eye in all the surrounding villages. Participating in this rite on one occasion had been an interesting experience, but under no circumstances did I wish to waste my time completing a circle in which I felt that I did not belong in the least. In spite of this I did not know how to refuse to accompany Maria as she desired.

When we entered Matilde's spacious kitchen the circle was already formed. The only light came from the leaping flames of the fire. As I took the place allotted me, I could not keep back an inopportune exclamation of surprise, breaking the quasi-sacred silence Matilde imposed on us. In the centre of the circle was no goat, but a woman: Elsa. She seemed very young, though later on I discovered that she was over thirty. She wore her clothes with extreme elegance and a certain unintentional carelessness. She had on a brown velvet jacket, in spite of the cold, a black sweater and an old faded blue denim skirt that reached to her ankles and revealed the dried out leather of a pair of country boots. She was standing in front of me and her eyes were shut. Her face, glowing both from the heat of the fire and from emotion, revealed that she had given herself over without reservation to this ceremony at which Matilde officiated. She did not make the slightest movement, nor did she open her eyes during all the time that the ceremony lasted. I observed her, amazed at the vegetable quiet that had taken possession of her whole body. Her delicate beauty held me unaware of my surroundings and totally absorbed. Faced with this inhuman immobility, I thought that perhaps she was not present here, amongst us, that in some way she had absented herself to another space, surrounded by the figures of an imaginary reality. I was not wrong, as I found out later, on getting to know her. Things half-seen acquired for her their most intense reality. And this, she said, was the meaning of life: intensity. It was unimportant that this should come more from fantasy than from reality.

Matilde let the three drops of oil slide from her fingers onto the water in the cup she held in her other hand. The circle immediately broke up. Within minutes everyone had left save Elsa and me, and at that moment I really felt like a shadow; for I am convinced that she did not even see me at her side as she peered at the surface of the water. The drops of oil had not spread, but outlined with precision the three points of a triangle. This was the worst of all possible presages, the sign that the ceremony had failed.

Elsa took leave briefly and left without giving any indication that she had been aware of my presence. In that atmosphere it suddenly appeared to me that some dark spell really did hang over her. She had made such an impression on me that I could not get her presence out of my mind for a large part of the night.

The next day I asked a few questions about her in the village. From the scant information I gleaned, I felt that it was impossible that anyone should live so solitary a life. She had come to these mountains before I had, but I had never come across her, not in the streets, nor in the shop, nor in the bar. She had come alone to rest and nurse a long, stubborn anaemia that she could not shake off. But later I learned that her illness, if such it could be called, was not anaemia but something else, more subtle and dangerous, which grew in the silence of this land, wrapping her in an immense sweetness and undermining her strength without her even seeming to care.

I decided to pay her a visit that same day. She lived in the lowest part of the village, in the last but one street, where only her house was inhabited. While I walked down the stony, slippery hills, I tried to imagine her there, surrounded by ruins and abandoned houses, among the vestiges of man's presence now dwindled to near non-existence. On reaching her door I knocked resolutely. I waited a short while, but, not hearing the slightest sound, knocked again insistently. An old woman was coming up the street with a bundle of kindling under her arm. Without my asking her anything she informed me that Elsa was in the house because she'd seen her go in on her way down to get her firewood. But as she could give me no idea how long ago that had been, I decided to look for her elsewhere.

I knocked at Matilde's door out of mere politeness as it was open. Nobody answered me so I started up the stairs, calling out, 'Can I come in?' to make my presence known in some way, and walked straight into the kitchen. They were both there, Elsa and she, sitting in front of the fire. Matilde greeted me with a smile of pleasure and straightaway invited me to sit down. Elsa, on the other hand, seemed put out and displeased by my visit. In spite of this I drew a chair up to the fire intending not to let myself be intimidated by her attitude. In the semi-darkness of the room, only the crackling of the flames and the wind whistling insistently from far off could be heard. I had a feeling that I had interrupted a conversation. After long minutes of silence, Matilde spoke in her slow, eager voice. She addressed herself amiably to me, aware of Elsa's resentment at my coming:

'Have you ever heard talk of the treasures that are hidden round here?'

'Now and then,' I replied, without being able to conceal a smile of incredulity.

'My father, poor man, lost his luck when he was young,' she said, still convinced of the existence of people who are touched one day by a mysterious and cruel fate.

If the favoured one allows himself to hesitate or to be afraid he loses his luck for ever. She told us that one evening her father was returning to the village at the hour between dusk and darkness, close to nightfall. He was a shepherd and he walked with his sheep, dressed the way shepherds used to be in those days, in a sheepskin coat and a Calañese hat. As he reached the Tajo del Molino he was startled by the sight of an enormous bull's tongue signalling frantically to him, flicking in and out of a tall rock, haloed in radiance such as he had never seen. He stopped to peer at this sign that his destiny had sent him. He knew, of course, the appropriate way to react to these magic beings that the Moors left behind as jealous guardians of their hidden treasures. All he had to do was to throw one of his sandals at the tongue and the rock would open and reveal to him a hidden treasure of incalculable riches. But, in spite of this, his terror at being swallowed by that gigantic tongue forced him to run from the place to which his luck had called him. He, who had never been afraid, fled like a coward. He told of a disembodied voice that called him by name as he hurried on, pushing his sheep before him, and said: 'You have lost your luck. Now you will have to work all your life. You will live in misery and die poorer still.'

And in case we, the outsiders, should doubt her tale, Matilde added that she too, on occasion, when she went to her gransparents' farm, had, herself, noticed the smell of boracic powder with which the Moors used to mark their hiding places. She said that she always fled and didn't stop running until that diabolical smell was completely effaced from her memory.

At times, listening to Matilde was to learn the history of the village, of its ancestors, of whatever they had believed they were living. It was a history in part manipulated by imaginary and cruel beings who seemed to amuse themselves playing with the misfortunes of the villagers. She never forgot her father. She said that he came back certain nights and crossed her bedroom several times, flitting from one wall to the other. On those occasions he took on the shape of a half moon, and gave off a faint glimmer to guide him in the dark. She used to wake up hearing his lamentations. They were terribly sad and became fainter and fainter until they faded away. She had never succeeded in talking to him. And, in spite of all the years gone by, she still kept a small oil lamp permanently lit. For here in these mountains death is sacred. It always has a face, a name, a history. The voices of the dead are never forgotten. They never entirely go away. In these mountains there are no other gods, no other saints than the souls. The living pray to them to look after their affairs, miracles come from them, they send signs from a different reality. To them prayers are addressed that storms and troubles may cease.

I used to look at Matilde as she talked to us in this vein; she seemed a recent arrival from a distant place to this world that she hardly knew, which surely seemed as strange to her as the unreal, dreamlike atmosphere with which she enveloped everything she named seemed to me.

'Very often,' she said, 'they tell you where there's a treasure. They say that if you dream the same thing three times, then it's true.'

Elsa, lost in other thoughts, suddenly exclaimed at this, 'Dreams are so strange!'

I looked at her speculatively, hoping she would go on, for those few words seemed the preamble to something that was seriously worrying her.

'Do you know anything about hypnosis?' she abruptly asked, addressing herself, I don't know why, solely to Matilde, as though I were not there too and giving her all my attention.

In spite of this, I considered myself included and before Matilde could think of anything to say, I intervened. Anyone who had heard me just then would have thought that the practice of hypnosis had been the driving force of my life. I recounted amazing, delirious happenings. They didn't even blink, surprised no doubt at finding something so unexpected in me. Elsa had bent forward to be closer to me, supporting her elbows on her knees. The most ingenious anecdote I told was one where I had endeavoured to use my so-called gift to a therapeutic end. It was about a young man with a stammer. I told them how I had slowly, not without difficulty, induced a hypnotic sleep that became deeper each time. Then I had led his mind to other moments of his life belonging to his earlier years. In this way I made him go back over his past until he reached the age of eleven. Then the miracle occurred: he spoke with the rhythm and fluidity of any normal person. His defect had disappeared. I told them that, of course, when he woke up his tongue still stumbled over every syllable he tried to utter, with no improvement whatsoever. I added that his problem had appeared precisely at eleven years old, immediately after an operation. I remember that this was the last case I recounted. In spite of their requests for more anecdotes I had run out of ideas. My imagination could think up no more. Obviously, everything I had been telling them was untrue. Not only had I never hypnotized anyone in my life, what was more, I had never even been interested in the subject, which I associated in my mind with tiers of wooden benches, a scant audience, damp earth on the ground, trumpet calls and the roll of a single drum. . . . I had only seen hypnosis practised in a circus and every time I heard the word the picture of a white rabbit appeared before my eyes, due no doubt to the fact that frequently the hypnotist was at the same time a conjuror, and either before or after plunging his assistant in a hypnotic trance he would pull a white rabbit out of his top hat.

I immediately realized that my invention had had the desired result: built a bridge to Elsa. From that moment on I discerned in her a certain liking for me. At least that was what I thought at the time; naively, for in actual fact all that Elsa saw in me was the necessary instrument to delve desperately into something that was mysteriously growing inside her, and which she fed as intensely as she could.

When I left she came with me. I had the impression there was something she wanted to say. But she walked silently beside me, making occasional remarks about the night. It was very cold and the wind still whistled down from the snow-covered peaks. As we reached the door of my house she invited me to go on to hers and have supper.

4

I followed Elsa to her house down steep streets, clumsily testing the stones and the mud, clutching the walls and judging every footstep with care for fear of falling. She had gone on ahead, I think without realizing it. I could hear her agile footsteps disappearing in the darkness, for the neighbourhood she lived in was abandoned and more or less uninhabited; not a single street lamp lit up its perilous slopes. The prolonged creaking of hinges told me that Elsa was opening a heavy door; we had at last reached her house. In the patio the dim light of one bulb revealed climbing plants on the walls, a marble table, wooden benches, a few broken chairs and a fountain of Granada tiles. Indoors I could hear her moving around with the ease of a cat. She was turning on, one by one, the five lamps that lit the spacious sitting room. At one end, next to a window, there was a small kitchen and at the other a fireplace where hot embers still glowed. She put on more logs and the fire immediately blazed up.

'Do you want to see the house?' she asked, and without waiting for my reply started on the tour.

The owner was a friend of hers who used it only occasionally. I followed her through rooms that differed one from the other, both in size and in decoration. They were situated on different floors and at different levels. From a small room as dark and austere as a monk's cell, we went into another large and colourful room, full of objects that seemed to have been brought together one by one with all the love of a collector. We ascended and descended various stairways: wide, narrow, made of slate or tiles, dark or well lit. . . . They were so disposed that they succeeded in confusing me and I no longer knew what was up and what was down, or whether we were on the top floor or in the cellar. We returned to the sitting room with its kitchen. The fire was still blazing but Elsa put on more logs. Then she went over to a vast wooden cabinet decorated with black tiles, containing a large collection of records. She chose one and put it on. She told me then that since her arrival in these mountains listening to music had been virtually her only occupation.

'Had you intended doing something else?' I asked eagerly, thinking that at last some sort of dialogue would be possible between us.

But I was wrong. She closed her eyes and, gently shrugging her shoulders in a gesture of indifference, replied: 'Not really. I can't think of anything I have to do.'

She then gave her full attention to the Handel sonata she had just chosen. The music imposed another long silence on us. I remember looking at her with indignation. I couldn't understand why she had invited me. As there was nothing else I could do, I devoted myself to observing her. Her face, flushed by the wind and the heat of the fire, reflected a profound sweetness, with which I could not sympathize as her attitude irritated me. On top of that, and in spite of myself, I felt hungry and thought of her invitation to supper – a detail that seemed to have slipped her mind entirely. In due course, at the end of the sonata, she relinquished her majestic immobility. Little by little I surrendered myself to the languid atmosphere she created with almost imperceptible movements of her body, with her expressions and, indeed, her words, which always revolved around herself. On several occasions she referred to her feeling for music as though it had been the only true vocation of her life. She regretted not having finished her studies at the Conservatory of Seville, the town where she was born. And since then, as the years passed, her frustration had increased. Now she did not play any instrument at all, but I do not remember ever having seen her in her house without the accompaniment of one of her favourite melodies. It was evident, as I understood later, that for her, music was the essential element in which her amorous dream world could come alive.

Suddenly, her movements became nervous. A new silence, strained this time, settled on her. I muttered various platitudes that fell on deaf ears as she seemed to take not the slightest interest in my presence. I was now sure that she had given up the idea of telling me whatever it was that I had been hoping for. Once again she stared into the fire, turned inwards on herself and oblivious of everything around her. Her extreme pallor seemed to reveal profound distress.

'At times it can be very hard living alone in a place as isolated as this.'

As I spoke, my words seemed trivial to me. They might be relevant to someone else, but not to Elsa. On hearing me, however, a flash of eagerness lit up her face and without taking her eyes from the fire, as though she addressed herself only to it, she spoke about solitude, or, to be precise, about her own solitude. She displayed such passion that I would have thought her chief ambition was never to set eyes on another human being for the rest of her life. Her desire for isolation was clearly defined by what seemed to be her vision of the world: on one side the whole of humanity, on the other, far, far away, herself alone. She said that in solitude, as the days, the months passed, everything became agreeable. All worries disappeared, losing themselves in a misty unreality. She assured me that she then acquired a quasi-innocent immediacy in her relationship with things. All her actions were pleasant but meaningless, whether washing dishes, writing, lighting the fire, listening to music, walking, reading, cooking, or quite simply, doing nothing. The most important things took on a quality of weightlessness, even of comedy. She said that little by little her perception was changing. She was discovering an extraordinary beauty in all the things that surrounded her, regardless of what they were. Her body was becoming as light as a cloud, and even the air seemed brilliant.

I listened to her in silence, convinced that her

words were not addressed to me. She was talking for herself and evidently did not expect any comments from me. In spite of this I enjoyed listening to her. Not only for what she revealed about herself, but also for her skill in making the most insignificant things seem interesting.

'Can I see you tomorrow?' she suddenly asked, without my having made the slightest move to leave.

'Yes . . . I suppose so,' I answered, disconcerted.

'Tomorrow evening?' she insisted.

'Yes – tomorrow evening will do,' and I looked at her, hoping for some sort of enlightenment.

'I've got to talk to you.'

'If you want to you can do so now.'

'No, I'd rather tomorrow.'

In her desire to postpone the conversation I had been hoping for, I discerned, rather put out, a manifest desire that I should leave. Of course it was late and I too was tired, but sending me off like that suddenly struck me as bad manners.

We said goodbye and I left her house wondering what it was that she wanted to tell me, something which, seemingly, she had not dared reveal in the course of my long visit. It was nearly dawn, the wind had died down and absolute silence had settled over the village. My torch lit up street corners, woodpiles, the inside of sheds, closed doors. . . . A few cats, eternally wary, crossed my path.

Next morning on waking up I felt an icy wind. My room was flooded. My first reaction was to stay in the raft that my bed had become and sleep on indefinitely under the shelter of the blankets. But the children were waiting for me at school, and though there were not many of them, they were all the village had. I was the only teacher and I couldn't miss classes. I already knew all the shortcomings of my house. I knew that I had to seal every gutter, every leak and every window through which the water poured in torrents every time there was a heavy rain. But the night before I had forgotten to put up the plastic sheeting that protected me.

That day I spent all my free time in the house repairing the night's disaster. I did not forget my appointment with Elsa although my curiosity had considerably abated. I reflected that up here in these mountains, the slightest detail took on ridiculous proportions. And each person acquired a relevance and an interest one would never have accorded them down below in the cities. It seemed that living here was like voyaging in a boat, adrift, lost on the sea, far from all coasts. No one knew where it was going and nobody seemed concerned about whether it would ever arrive in port.

When I met Elsa I was suffering for the first time from that sort of stagnation to which everyone who settles here permanently seems prone. It is a passing but cyclic malady, the other face of the elation that these mountains provoke when you first see them. The serenity that I thought I had so easily attained suddenly became boredom that kept me drowsing in the warmth of the fire for hours on end or drifting round the streets half asleep. At such times I only moved when forced by automatic routine. The hopeless silence of the mountains and of the whole village drove me to wander endlessly around the icy, empty streets, muffled up in a black scarf like one more of the old women who glided along like sombre ghosts, wrapped in their black shawls and permanently in mourning. With alarm I discerned in myself the signs of a dangerous lethargy, signs of a vegetal life beginning to invade me, cancelling out whatever pleasant impressions a landscape might arouse, for in spite of its beauty, the landscape too seemed to immure itself in lethargic silence.

This was perhaps why I forced myself not to let my curiosity concerning Elsa, and her improbable presence in the village, abate. So, before the sun set behind the Tajo Gallego, I set out for her house. Something there did succeed in arousing my interest, a faint emotion that sprang from the strange atmosphere, born of the extraordinary house, the music Elsa chose, Elsa herself: the dreamy air that surrounded each of her gestures, her melodious voice, her silences, her glance wandering always on planes of unreality.

5

The door of Elsa's house was open. I went in without knocking and found her in the living room. She was drinking tea sitting close to the hearth. I noticed that she was expecting me, for on the tray next to the teapot was a second cup. As soon as I sat down I started talking about this and that: the flooding of my house, the importance that rain, sun, mist and wind took on here. I did not intend to put up with any more silences between us. She, of course, didn't listen to me. She sat so motionless that she could have been a painted figure, arrested for ever in time. It was evident that her attention was wandering who knows where, distant and detached from my words and from everything that these walls that housed her contained.

Suddenly, without even looking at me and without giving any explanation, she said: 'I want you to hypnotize me.'

'When?' I asked, feigning indifference, as though her suggestion had not surprised me; as though I did not know full well that I was incapable of doing anything of the sort.

'Now,' she answered decidedly, but in the same easy tone I suppose she might have used to ask me to tea.

I tied myself up purposely in various excuses I can now no longer remember, but which were clumsily intended to show how difficult such an extraordinary undertaking was. I think I said among other things that I would have to know her a bit better before attempting an experiment that might be harmful to her. Even if I failed to discourage her entirely, I hoped at least to postpone the moment. But without paying any attention to me she rose and walked across the sitting room. With one hand she stopped the pendulum of a wall clock. She couldn't bear its ticking. I could not understand how she was able to hear it through the music. She sat down again next to me and looked at me for the first time since my arrival; concentrating as always on her own thoughts and ignoring mine, she said, 'It's about my dreams.'

She started remembering out loud the pictures of a story that recurred in her dreams; dissolving sometimes and reappearing at others with an insistence that frightened and attracted her. It seemed to summon her to some incorporeal place and her intention was precisely to return to this dream world and interrogate it. The same person always appeared: Agustín Valdés. And always the same outcome: his madness at her death. Her memory retained precise images belonging to the same sequence of events: the ochre colour of the earth on a path, a high wall made of large stones, the black frockcoat and white ruffled shirt worn by Agustín running like a madman behind the coffin that enclosed her body. It was borne on the shoulders of various people whom she had not yet recognized. Suddenly someone seized Agustín roughly as he started to shake the coffin, trying to open it. He wanted to recover Elsa's body, denying her death in loud cries, trying to stop them from burying her. On either side a file of faceless people followed them, weightless and silent like penitents in a nocturnal procession.

On other occasions she was running along the same wall from which a man jumped down, forcing her to stop. He was wrapped in a black cloak. It was night and she could never see him clearly, but in her dream she thought that it was Agustín Valdés.

Elsa spoke as though she thought these pictures might have substance in some actual space, in another time.

'Who is Agustín Valdés?' I asked.

She didn't answer.

'Do you know him well?' I insisted.

'No. Hardly at all. I've only seen him twice. But in my dreams. . . .'

'Did anything special happen?' I asked.

'No. Actually, nothing happened.'

Her thin, childlike hands moved restlessly, twining in the black curly hair that fell to her shoulders. I thought then that certain diseases could sometimes reveal themselves in a face, disguised as rapture or passion, and also that people would surely say that someone like Elsa was 'mad'. But now, whenever I think of her I feel a deep respect for her words, her hope, her suffering, her melancholy, her lack of interest in life, her helplessness . . . all strung on the thread of a sentiment that was perhaps only love of Love. For now I am convinced that it was love, not sickness, that imparted its radiance to her. And each time I read in her notebook those words that were weaving love and despair at the same time, I feel I am touching an almost sacred reality. It started thus:

Is it really true that I have seen you only
twice? I couldn't say how many times we
have met, you and I, nor how many hours of
my life I have devoted to you. Your presence
in my solitude is as intense as when I saw
you opposite me on the other side of a café
table; not to mention seeing you in all those
dreams, which are engraving on my mind
something resembling a common past of
many years. Now I know your gestures, your
anger, your laughter, your attitudes, your
silences. . . . Tell me, can a simple dream
give such intensity to a feeling? How is this
love possible that seems to have had no
beginning? From the first time I saw you, I
loved you already with a long-standing love.
This feeling is as real as the heat of the sun
or the cold of the snow. Perhaps it is more
important to know the way you dress, the
food you like, or the little bad habits that
mar everyday life. Are you all that? I know
that you are what I have seen and what I
now dream. Sometimes I ask myself how
dreams can weave a story that has taken hold
of me more than life itself. Or perhaps they
are my life? They affect me more than the

events called real. I ask myself where these pictures that unite us so intimately in dreams come from. I ask myself with bewilderment, wrapped in a sort of spell that is so sweet that I would not exchange it for anything in the world.

Only a few months had gone by since Elsa's first visit to Barcelona. She had gone there at the insistent invitation of an old friend. At that time she had just broken off a love affair, which, according to her brief comments, had been going on for years, tormenting her and tearing her away again and again from whatever activity she undertook. On the eve of her departure a friend had asked her to deliver a letter to a colleague of his. The unknown recipient was Agustín Valdés. This intervention of fate in her story filled her with excitement. All she knew about him was that he was a teacher of philosophy, as was his friend, and as she herself had been for as long as she had been able to bear it. She took the letter without paying too much attention to the reasons given for such a request. He could say what he liked, she considered it an impertinence and a bore and, quite evidently, unnecessary. In spite of this she promised to deliver it if she found a suitable moment.

She had to phone Agustín Valdés several times before contacting him. At last she had her first conversation with him. She wrote the following about it in her notebook:

Later, when memory restored the emotion
that sprang up in me, suddenly,
treacherously, unnoticed at the time, I knew
that at the very moment when I heard your
voice for the first time 'this' had begun,
which is more than love, but to which I still
cannot give a name.

Agustín arranged a meeting and she asked him: 'How shall I recognize you? I've never seen you.'

He answered: 'I'm of medium height, normal appearance, with dark hair, black eyes and a bushy moustache. And you?'

'Me?' she said anxiously, startled by his question and unable to think of any way of describing herself. 'I'll have a white envelope in my hand.'

Did I really see you that time, when I
entered the café and you approached me,

silent, almost shy? Did I see you then, when, shaken by a violent emotion, I murmured some formula or other of introduction or greeting to justify my presence before you? No, no, it couldn't have been then, for in those moments all I could do was tremble. Afterwards, for a whole long day, nothing existed for me other than our next meeting. You yourself had fixed it for the following evening. During that long wait I was nothing but dread and hope. It was then, in solitude, that I really saw you. You were etched on my thoughts, on the darkness behind my closed eyelids, on my breathing, on my heartbeats. . . .

6

Elsa had fixed the hour and the date of our first hypnotic session without consulting me. I arrived unintentionally late. I found her, as usual, sitting in front of the fire listening to music and totally inactive. She hardly gave me time to greet her. She wanted to start immediately. All words or actions she saw simply as obstacles delaying her arrival in that other place where her dreams happened and where she hoped to meet Agustín Valdés. I, on the other hand, wanted to put off the experiment for as long as possible. I asked her to make me a cup of tea to warm me up as it was very cold. In actual fact I needed at least a few minutes to improvise my farce and lead up to the inevitable failure without giving myself away too stupidly. I had the feeling that Elsa was totally unconventional; she never pretended, she jumped straight into reality, almost tripping over it. I didn't succeed in persuading her to have a cup of tea with me. I drank several cups on my own and finally decided to start the session. To begin with I proposed lighting a candle. Night was falling, and, oddly, the living room lamps were not yet lit. The fire in the hearth gave off a faint light in which I felt safe. I held the candle in front of Elsa's face, telling her to keep looking at the small flame, while I moved it from side to side. She followed it obediently with her eyes, hardly blinking, while she listened to my voice inviting her, with no conviction whatever, to relax ever more and more. After ten minutes or so her eyelids began to droop and at last she shut her eyes completely as though she really had fallen into a deep sleep. In that dim light her hieratic features seemed those of a sphinx.

Then, wishing to wake her up, I said firmly: 'Now I shall count to ten. When I've finished you won't be able to move your right arm, even though you try with all your strength.'

In those ten seconds that passed slowly but anxiously, one thought alarmed me: what if Elsa really were hypnotized, even though that had not been my intention? She looked so stiff and strange that I had an urge to shake her and tell her of my imposture. But it was not necessary, for as I reached ten she lifted her arm with complete ease, disobeying my unconvincing order. She opened her eyes and with a gesture of annoyance informed me that she hadn't even gone to sleep.

'I don't know what can have happened,' I murmured, relieved. 'Maybe lack of practice. I gave all this up years ago.'

'You can try with another method,' she said.

She rose as though prompted by a sudden inspiration and disappeared into the house to return shortly after and show me a platinum ring set with diamonds. She strung it on a length of thread and let it fall in a pendulum movement in front of the still lighted candle. I dreaded her asking me to go on, or rather, to start anew. I had made up my mind to refuse. But it wasn't necessary. A sudden discouragement, a sort of sadness, made her gather up the thread and the ring in her hands. She sat down, staring at the emptiness of the floor at her feet. Seeing this, I blurted out a few questions that would have struck anyone else as indiscreet, but she found in them sufficient incentive to regain her lost eagerness. It seemed that just evoking Agustín Valdés, clothing him in the reality of words, sufficed for her to feel that in some way she was fulfilling her love. In fact, words were the only earthly material with which she could build her strange story and feed an emotion whose reality, regardless of where it came from, could not be denied. Her answers revealed to me the enormous folly that she alone had constructed. I found myself, to my amazement, offering the words and advice that would have occurred to anybody, trying to distract her from the intensity with which she was surrendering herself to what seemed to me to be a fantasy out of all proportion. When I questioned her about Agustín Valdés she got involved in detailed descriptions and it took me a while to discover that she was always talking about the other Valdés, the one who appeared in her dreams. It was evident that in her mind the possible differences between the two had been wiped out. I also learned that the meeting he himself had arranged did not take place. She had been there, in the café he had chosen, sitting at the last table in a corner of the room, confidently expecting him, denying the passing of time, anticipating him anxiously in every silhouette outlined against the glass panes by the lights of the nighttime city. He had made an appointment with her and had not kept it, leaving her prey to a chain of conjectures that forced her to phone him again. Suppose his failure to come had been due to a misunderstanding?

Had he been waiting for her in a different place? Or had some unforeseen event stopped him from coming? Perhaps at this very moment, upset at not having met her, he was impatiently waiting for her to phone.

In an unconscious gesture, due perhaps to momentary distraction, Elsa rolled up the thread she had strung through the ring and threw it into the fire. Then, slipping the ring on her finger, she showed me her outstretched hand; it was far too thin for the jewel. She told me that she had inherited it from a great-aunt whom she hardly knew. And, without attaching further importance to it, she continued with her story; a story in which, in spite of her eagerness, I detected ultimate, inescapable disaster, though whether she realized it I couldn't say.

That night she waited for Agustín Valdés until the café emptied and she was politely requested to leave. It was closing time. In her notebook she had written:

Night itself was falling on me, darkening my eagerness. The streets were empty and a gentle rain silently soaked through my clothes, my hair, mingling with my tears, for

I was crying bitterly, without even asking myself what was happening to me. Through my tears my eyes looked blindly in every direction. I still hoped to meet you. I was overcome by a measureless desire to see you again.

She phoned Agustín and he apologized sincerely: acute toothache had prevented him from keeping their appointment. He added, moreover, that he would like to see her before she returned to Madrid. They agreed then on a further meeting in the same café.

When you came up to me and greeted me with a polite kiss, I realized that my voice was shaking, as were my hands, my hair, my whole body. Once again, I could not stop trembling for many minutes. In that state the most trivial things took on a mysterious meaning in my eyes. For instance, you were waiting for me at the very same corner table where, the night before, I had asked myself whether I had really seen you, whether it was true that you had made an appointment with me and might arrive at any moment.

They had only managed to exchange a few words in a strained silence when Agustín Valdés asked her, 'Do you know anything about the cabbala?'

Elsa, disconcerted, for she knew next to nothing about it, handed him, in answer, the book that she had brought with her, *Considerations on Sin, Hope, and the True Way* by F. Kafka. The preface stated that the author had belonged to the Hasidic sect, a cabbalist group that had appeared in Poland in the seventeenth or eighteenth century, she couldn't remember which. Agustín read some of the aphorisms to be found in the first pages. From this sprang a long conversation about which Elsa subsequently wrote:

I cannot ever remember human speech
having been so fulfilling. I still cannot
explain what happened there between you
and me. Later, when you went to telephone,
I opened the book and read the first
aphorism I met. I can remember that it was
number seventeen and said: 'I had never
been here. Next to her a star shines more
brightly than the sun.' And this apparent
coincidence was the first clear, undeniable

presage of a love I was beginning to acknowledge. I had no particular reason to return to Madrid, but all the same I decided to leave the next day, to your apparent dismay. That expression of regret, perhaps no more than a reflex of politeness, moved me to such an extent that it drove me to flee in terror. For it really was flight, now I know it. But in spite of that, even though your memory had faded from my mind, I returned to Barcelona months later with the sole intention of seeing you, as though I was obeying an old desire, now nearly forgotten. You told me you had no time free and I wandered all day through the streets, resentful and suspicious, wondering whether you were not just making an excuse for not seeing me. Perhaps because of this, when at last you made an appointment with me, showing, indeed, considerable interest in our meeting, a powerful, violent attraction overwhelmed me. I had never felt anything like it. Once again, you failed to turn up, but this time I did not suffer, rather the contrary; I was suddenly flooded by an unjustifiable happiness. Overcome by delight

I attributed your failure to come to a hidden
destiny that, somehow or other, by
preventing our meeting, was bringing us
closer together. But I was wrong. When
I phoned to ask the reason for your non-
appearance, your answer was pitiless: 'I was
busy and the time passed. I suddenly
remembered, but by then it was too late.' A
long tearful complaint broke from my lips.
I listened to my own voice as though it were
coming from outside me, as though it were
not I who spoke. I felt powerless to hold
back the absurdity that you, without
knowing it, had let loose in me.

'No, I won't phone you,' Elsa had answered
when he asked her, offhandedly, to phone him
some other time. 'I shall stay here in Barcelona; I
shall live here, but I'll never phone you.'

'Well, that's all right by me,' answered
Agustín, exasperated.

'I'm normal!' she then screamed, trying to
hold back her sobs. 'I'm not a monster! I'm not a
monster!'

For, when they first met, Agustín had said,
half jokingly, that she aroused in him an

incomprehensible fear. And those words that she had listened to, almost with pleasure at the time, suddenly took on overtones of cruelty that she had not previously noticed and revealed to her the sole reason for his absences.

You cannot imagine how I saw myself at that moment. I was something shapeless and repugnant, I was a well full of horrors and things that threatened me. I was monstrosity's very self. And from that now incomprehensible pit I gabbled on without control. Now all I can remember is that desperate cry that came back like a refrain between my moans: 'I'm not a monster! I'm not a monster!'

Agustín Valdés gave no answer to Elsa's protestations.

'Are you listening to me?' she asked in despair. 'Are you there?'

There did not seem to be anyone at the other end of the line. Only silence. At last she hung up, doubting that he had listened to her.

There is no point now in telling you about

my suffering, my absurd tears; about the
days I stayed on in Barcelona, wandering
through the streets, foolishly seeing you in
every passer-by. How often I ran to catch up
with someone who, from the back, might
have been you. I wandered from one place to
another, suffering from your absence all
through the city.

Between the last pages of the Kafka book Elsa
had brought with her, she found a postcard she
had forgotten there a good while back. It was a
reproduction of Paolo Uccello's *Saint George and
the Dragon*. It showed a woman in front of a sombre cave from which she seemed to have just
emerged, leading the legendary monster on a
rope. Saint George, from his horse, wounds it
with his lance.

. . . finding it just then was another
coincidence that fed my hope. I knew that
our meeting would not be lost in oblivion.
I even succeeded in believing that fate was
keeping us united in some mysterious way.

Elsa then sent the postcard to Agustín Valdés

after writing on the back: 'We are not the ones who pull the strings of "reality". It is others who do so, as we are told in the *Iliad* – which happened in Troy. Love.'

And underneath she added: 'Wouldn't you like to be as brave as Saint George?'

7

After several days without our seeing each other, Elsa came to visit me one night. It was very late and she came in without knocking. She sat down next to me, uttered some sort of greeting and immediately started talking, as though there had been no interval between our last meeting and this one. She went on with her conversation, always about herself, as though four days had not elapsed, as though, during that time, I had not endeavoured to hide, avoiding her part of the village and even absenting myself from my own house in case she thought of visiting me. I did not wish to lend myself again to that pretence at hypnosis. I did not wish to go on deceiving her, and I couldn't see any chance of succeeding, for I was quite convinced of my inability to plunge anyone into such a state. But, in spite of all this, I had ended up going down to Orgiva, a rather distant village but larger than ours, with the intention of buying a book on hypnosis in the only bookshop there. I remember saying, 'Whatever you've got, anything will do,' but they had nothing.

This time Elsa actually talked to me, leaving moments of silence that were requests for my comments on her words.

'Sometimes,' she was saying, 'I shut my eyes and I can perceive within me something bottomless, without limits, something that I could call a mystery. I think it is there that all these dreams about Agustín Valdés come from, and from there also come the emotions that wake me up.'

When she stopped talking I lowered my eyes to avoid meeting hers. I listened to her voice as to a strange sound with power to arrest time and to create all around us an atmosphere in which nothing seemed to exist except the figment her words conjured up. She was so absorbed in the story that had now become reality for her that my anxiety seemed unimportant, and to my surprise I found myself once again assuming the role she imposed on me. This time I was the one who brought up the idea of hypnosis. I even went so far as to apologize sincerely for not having been to visit her. It was evident that my attitude affected her very little as she had come quite decided that we should try the experiment again.

Nevertheless, she said:

'I do know that you don't want to hypnotize me – I have noticed it. It may even seem to you just a ridiculous game between us.'

And I thought then, without saying so, that perhaps it was exactly that: a ridiculous game we shared. Elsa and I were both outsiders in the village and this brought us together. Our isolation gave me a feeling close to solidarity with her. We both lived on the edge of that small group, for in spite of the apparent simplicity of the villagers, their lives were circumscribed by a continual ceremony; their days ran on in a succession of rites that were inaccessible to us. I thought that in some way I was cast to play out our own ceremony with her.

'We'll try once again,' I finally agreed.

'Now?' she asked.

'What, just like that . . . so suddenly?' I murmured, hedging.

'Why not?' she said, showing me the diamond ring she had just taken out of her bag.

She had already prepared it, tying both ends of a thread on either side of the setting. Then, for the first time, the feelings I had previously labelled, without saying so, adolescent fantasy at its worst, began to excite my curiosity: I wanted to peer into that mist of hers, a mist from which seemed to spring such incessant pictures of love and death.

Elsa, suddenly still as a rock, endeavoured not to blink, concentrating on the pendulum swing of the ring that I held in front of her watering eyes. I listened to my own voice, firm now, ordering her to sink gradually to depths unknown to both of us. When at last I realized that she really was hypnotized, I wanted to wake her up immediately, to escape from someone whose identity at that moment I no longer knew. I tried to compose myself and started asking questions so trite as to be positively nauseous, as though they could allay the fears that beset me.

'In front of you there is a black screen,' I said; 'concentrate on it. Can you see anything?'

Elsa did not answer. I had to repeat the same words over several times, trying to create a visible screen behind her closed eyelids. At last she said: 'I can see Agustín.'

'Describe him,' I ordered.

'His eyes are black, his face pale, his hair is dark, as is his moustache. He has lowered his eyes. He's looking at the ground. Behind him, very far away, I can see some pointed towers.'

'How is he dressed?'

'He's wearing a dark brown jacket, it looks like velvet, trousers of the same colour and a white shirt with ruffles and lace. His clothes are not of this century.'

'What is he doing?'

'He has started to walk. He's going towards the towers. I have never seen those towers.'

'Is he in a town?'

'Yes.'

'Do you know it?'

'No.'

'In what country is it?'

'Germany.'

'What is it called?'

Elsa did not answer. I waited a few minutes, then insisted again: 'In what part of Germany is it?'

'In the south.'

'In what year are you seeing it?'

She said nothing. She did not seem to have heard me.

'Can you see Agustín?' I then asked.

'I can see Eduardo.'

'Eduardo?'

'Yes. Eduardo is walking towards the towers.'

'Who is Eduardo? Is he Agustín?'

More than ten minutes passed. Elsa remained motionless, seemingly halted or lost in some recess of that extraordinary memory of hers, a memory that I was evoking with my questions. I did not even ask myself whether these pictures had belonged to some reality. All I knew was that fragments of a story floated around her and I wanted to put them together again.

'Now the screen in front of you is blank,' I murmured. 'You are going to see a date written on it. Can you tell me what it is?'

'Eighteen sixty-four' – this time she answered immediately.

'Can you see anything else?'

She was silent, so I asked, 'Who is Eduardo? Do you know him?'

'Yes. Yes, I know him,' she said emphatically.

'Now it is night,' I suggested. 'You are walking alone next to a wall. You're in the country. A man jumps down from it and blocks your way. He frightens you. Who is it?'

'Eduardo.' As she pronounced the name her face was drawn as though in real alarm.

'What's happening?' I insisted several times.

Instead of answering me she said, 'Ask me what he's saying.'

'Oh, come on!' I protested with annoyance. 'Are you having me on?'

That immediately broke up the scene, a scene in which I was participating as much as she was. I suspected that her trance was perhaps no more than a pretence put on for her own benefit.

'So,' I said. 'You're awake.'

She did not react to my question and I was on the point of verifying whether she really was sunk in unknown depths, when suddenly a blast of icy air swept through the room preventing further questions. Someone appeared without knocking. It was Matilde. She carefully opened the door and remained very quiet, framed in the doorway, her arms folded and her feet together, as she would have done on her own doorstep to indulge in lengthy gossip with other women as old as herself. A stray cat slipped in with the cold and in one jump reached the kitchen bench. Matilde tapped several times on the glass panes of the door, unnecessarily announcing her presence. I ran for the cat whilst greeting her and threw it back into the cold. Then I invited her in unenthusiastically, hoping she would refuse.

'Elsa is asleep,' I whispered close to her.

Matilde resolutely picked up a wickerwork chair and brought it to the warmth of the hearth. She placed herself somewhat further back from the fire than we were and stretching out her arms held out her open hands to the blazing logs.

'It's as cold as death,' she said, whilst looking at us with undisguised curiosity. Then she folded her arms and waited as any spectator would have done. She had a wonderful capacity for feeling herself to be invisible and hiding behind long silences, as though it were not necessary to say anything just because she happened to be with other people; as though it sufficed to look the way she did at such times, like someone alone on the other side of a screen.

Of course she did not believe that Elsa sitting there so stiffly was asleep, especially as the expression on her face did not go with deep sleep, but rather suggested someone very much awake with eyes alert behind closed eyelids.

'Now would you please be so kind as not to say anything for a few minutes,' I curtly requested. 'I'm going to wake her up.'

I gave her no further explanation. I did not find it necessary to enlighten her as to what I was

going to wake her up from, for I was quite sure
that Matilde already knew what the two of us
were doing.

'Wait,' she said, rather anxiously. 'Ask her if
he wears spectacles.'

'He? Who?'

'That man, the one from Barcelona.'

'She doesn't have to be hypnotized for that.
Ask her yourself afterwards.'

It was clear that, without consulting me, Elsa
had informed her of the session she had decided
would take place that night. What could she have
told her, I asked myself, annoyed at Matilde's
intrusion in this extraordinary story. And, above
all, what could she have understood of the
amorous lethargy into which Elsa was sinking?

'Well then, ask her something else,' she said,
with a childish enthusiasm that struck me as
totally out of place. The fact was that I did not
really know what to do, caught up in the confusion that the two of them had created for me.

'You're still thinking about the evil eye, aren't
you?' I said, inopportunely, and with deliberate
animosity. For I had already heard her, in a
different context, say that spectacle lenses
reduced the evil of those who had that power in

their eyes. Her only answer was to shrug her shoulders and raise her eyebrows in a placid gesture of resignation.

I got up and going over to Elsa shook her gently.

'Wake up, it's all over,' I said drily, suspecting that her rigidity could have been put on.

But I was mistaken. She moved under my hand like a lifeless doll. Faced with the fear of not being able to bring her back into this world, and not having foreseen that this return might present a problem, I decided to use the same method I had seen used at the circus.

'I'm going to count to ten,' I whispered shakily in her ear. 'When I've finished I'll clap my hands and you'll be back here again, awake, just as usual.'

And that is exactly what happened. Elsa reappeared at last among us, smiling as though she had just awakened from a peaceful sleep.

8

An opaque greyness floated over the road, hiding the village and the green countryside, ashen and devoid of light: the greyness of mist at twilight. It settled on us, surrounding us and imprisoning us in a limbo out of time. Elsa was wearing a sailor's pea-jacket and the same denim skirt I had first seen her in. The cold had entered every fibre of her body and she was shivering from head to toe. I could hear her teeth chattering behind her purple wool scarf. But in spite of this, it was she who had insisted on taking a walk along the road. She said the mist fascinated her. I had run into her in the shop, right on the outskirts of the village. We walked downhill with quick strides trying to get warm, but the cold clung to us like a second skin that we could not shake off. I suggested turning back, alleging that I must correct my pupils' belated examination papers. Once again I felt that she was not listening to me.

I stopped and said: 'Elsa, when I talk to you

about things that interest me, what do you think about?'

She looked at me, smiling, surprised that I had noticed her lack of attention.

'I'm sorry,' she said. 'Something different every time, I suppose. I can't help it.'

'You shouldn't mull over your obsessions,' I said tartly, offended by her constant failure to listen. 'You're always somewhere else.'

'Well, what does it matter anyway?' she answered calmly, shrugging her shoulders at my reproof.

We retraced our steps in silence, walking slowly up the hill. On reaching the village we went into the bar. It smelled of damp firewood, of cold and of tobacco smoke. Men – for women did not go there – sat at the tables round the stove. Some played cards; others, absent and silent, stared into nothingness. We sat down at the far end, protected by the semi-darkness, away from their prying eyes. The light of the one and only bulb that hung from the ceiling hardly reached our corner.

'And what's more,' I went on, intending to jolt her into a different frame of mind, away from the dedicated obsession she brought to her dreams, 'this love story, or whatever it is, ended pretty quickly in real life. Or rather, according to what you've told me, never even got round to starting. Isn't that so?'

'What do you mean by "real life"?'

'Just what anyone would understand by reality. It's very simple.'

'Too simple. Reality is never simple,' she answered seriously.

'All right,' I went on, 'I mean that absolutely nothing at all happened.'

'You mean we didn't go to bed together? Don't be so stupid!'

'I'm not referring to anything specific. But in your case . . . the truth is you met just twice, and over a cup of coffee at that.'

'I don't expect you to understand a word of what I've told you till now. Neither you nor anyone else. But in spite of everything, my love does exist.'

The word 'reality' worried Elsa. I'd noticed it on numerous occasions. It had the power to provoke a disagreeable feeling of unease. Perhaps it suggested something too vague, ambiguous and incomprehensible: the patterns of a kaleidoscope, ever changing, never to be repeated, always out of reach. When she spoke of her love it was as though hers was the only one or the first one in the whole history of humanity; as though the experience of others could offer her no guidance. Yet, in spite of my words, I knew that her love was real and inordinately intense; powerful enought to feed upon itself and upon her prodigious imagination. Sometimes I endeavoured to make her see a little sense, but gradually I myself became a participant in her amorous rites and surrendered myself, just as she did, to the pursuit of an imaginary story that seemed to have happened, or that might yet happen, in a mythical time, in a different space.

Night had fallen when we left the bar. We only met a few stray cats as we walked down the steep streets of the village. We could hear our careful footsteps resounding on the paving stones of the road. When we reached the village square, Elsa took a white envelope out of her bag and asked me to wait a moment. I stood under a cattle shed and watched her walk through the mist to the post box. She slipped her letter into it and came back slowly, almost gliding along. Her eyes were shut and she was moved by something close to ecstasy. That afternoon she had been walking in the fields beyond the last houses of the village, when suddenly, the earth itself offered her an unexpected gift: a fragile flower grew from it. It seemed embroidered on the air in fine threads of grey-blue and green. She knew its name. She said it came from England and was called 'love-in-a-mist'. There were many of them and she examined them all carefully several times to find the most beautiful one. As she returned home, she said, the flower she held in her hand gave off the warmth of a living being. She put it in the envelope she had just posted with a short note: 'Dear Agustín, I'm giving you this flower because it is called "love-in-a-mist". Do you like it?'

As I listened to her, I had silently to admit that the love that possessed her day and night was the most real I had ever witnessed in my life. What else could one think of that almost sacred intensity with which she devoted herself to these insignificant actions? And I still believe that her emotion really was love each time I reread her notebook and discover entries such as this:

In September I went to Venice. It was more than a voyage, it was a pilgrimage to forgetfulness – even though, at the time, I flattered myself, when alone, that I had killed my desire to see you and wiped your presence from my memory thanks to my own willpower. I knew that if I made one last effort I would succeed in erasing you from existence. And my desire then was that you should never have existed. So I set out, fleeing from you, without yet knowing that though you were disappearing from my memory it was only to sink to a more dangerous level, to the hidden labyrinths of my subconscious, to emerge later and drag me in pursuit of your shadow to imaginary scenes, to this tower of wind, where now I know I am you prisoner.

When I boarded the *vaporetto* that goes up the Grand Canal of Venice, I knew nothing of that strange appointment in the very heart of the night – which you kept this time – in the damp *pension* close to Saint Mark's Square, where I had taken a room. I don't know how long I stayed there in the darkness, without moving, stiff with cold, listening to the echoes of the water gnawing at the age-old stone. You did not exist for me in those moments. Perhaps it was then that I reached the most perfect forgetfulness; there, alone, in that strange bedroom in a foreign city, far from everything that made up my life. There too I was overtaken by an inexplicable terror. A terror that came from the water flowing everywhere through the city. I remember crying tears of anguish without knowing what was happening to me. At last I decided to go out and meet whatever it was that terrified me so absurdly. Once in the street, that other Venice revealed itself, impossible and ghostly. Full of shadowy images that breathed and undulated in stony hollows reflected in the watery mirror of the canals. From them the solid façades rose up and in them their foundations were sunk, like ghosts opening their eyes to the night and exhaling a frozen breath that clung to my whole body.

When I returned to the *pension*, pierced through with damp and cold but free of thought, I slept at last – though I still don't know whether what immediately happened to me really was sleep. The images of my dream had the same solidity as the stones of the streets I had wandered through, losing myself until dawn. I suddenly found myself in a different place – I do not know whether in sleep or in some sort of wakefulness. It was then that I really met you as I had not succeeded in doing before in Barcelona. We embraced, you and I, immersed in a sea that had no other limits than the emptiness of the sky. I knew that I loved you with an unknown intensity. But suddenly I saw an enormous eagle circling above us. I can still remember its black wings getting bigger as it approached me. It was coming for me; I knew as soon as I saw it. It held me prisoner in its claws, pulling me from your arms as you tried to hold me back. To the sorrow of losing you was added my fear that you would discover my monstrosity: for I was not really a woman, but a siren. How long did that anguished flight to the heavens last, revealing to your eyes my monstrous body, the sign of a fatal interdiction to our union?

The next morning I walked round Venice in the aura of your love, for we belonged together in that dream in which, rather than sleeping, I seemed to awake to a mysterious sentiment that the light of day could not

dim. I no longer wanted to forget. I loved
you with a new fullness and in the warmth
of that love I lived all those days. The
shadow of your love floated over the whole
city. Should I ever return there, I would not
find a single corner, bridge, canal, square or
church that was not a precious reminder of
you, Agustín, you who in the meantime went
on living unaware of my passion. During the
long walks I took, you went with me in that
other element that was not sleep nor yet
waking, but something else, magic and ours.
Every night I went to a concert and every
melody became a meeting place for us. You
love music just as I do, you told me so
yourself. And in this way, surrendering
myself to the exaltation it aroused in me,
I allowed your shadow to come to life, as
inapprehensible as music or the water where
Venice was slowly sinking. Later, when I was
back in Madrid, with no hope of seeing you
again, your incorporeal presence took form
as it appeared again in my dreams
throughout the winter. Without my realizing
it you were quietly gliding to that realm
beyond time that we harbour in some corner

of our inner selves. You became a dream and grew, feeding on my days, on my awareness, stealing my every initiative, my hours of sleep; putting a real distance between me and anything that was not you. I had become a lost wandering ghost, pursuing your shadow which had become my only reality. The need to touch you in some way, to prove that you really existed, drove me to sending my second message. At that time, writing was the only possible means of getting nearer to you. It is possible that you would have answered if I had given you my address, but secret fears held me back. Two weeks have already passed and I feel I am standing on the threshold of a dream, ready to cross over and enter it with my eyes wide open, with my entire body. I still remember what I wrote. I have said it over silently to myself so many times, seeking within myself the echoes it might have aroused in you, trying to be you again and again, guessing your feelings and your thoughts, removing from you anything that is not known to me. Here are the words I wrote for you: 'There are black ghosts dancing in the blue of the night and you were out of reach behind a pane of blue glass. Blue were my sadness and your shadow, blue a deep tearless sorrow, blue your silence in my suffering. And your eyes . . . boundless black seas lost to my hope.'

9

Around the village streets and houses one never heard a song, a radio or a guitar. A dark heaviness hovered oppressively over the villagers; I only ever heard odd words, short sentences, snatches of abruptly interrupted conversation. Matilde was different. She only had two or three friends, who kept a respectful distance. The other inhabitants of the village were afraid of her. Nobody doubted that someone who can exorcize the evil eye can also cast it. She was a slight woman of medium height and very thin. Like so many other women here, she was born at the turn of the century, but her skin, furrowed by deep wrinkles, was illuminated and rejuvenated by the extraordinary intensity of her eyes. Her figure seen from afar, thanks to the energy and agility of her movements, was that of a young woman. She habitually kept her opinions to herself and was cautious in the brief comments she occasionally made. She used the words of others as an excuse to set the train of her memories in motion. She would then talk comfortably on, lost in an intemporal 'before' that was still alive in her memory. Her words created, evoked and invented a strange and cruel world that had really existed around here in other times. She lived in the kitchen of her house and slept in a small room next to it. I don't think she ever used the rest of the house. I never managed to see it, although she told me it was all perfectly furnished. A few days after her intrusion into our hypnotic session I went to visit her. She had a practical, close to the earth side which expressed itself chiefly in commerce. I had already been in her kitchen several times to buy eggs from her chickens or milk from her goats, for it served on occasion as a shop. Once she even offered to kill a hen or a rabbit for us, as she did for some of the villagers. Elsa refused and I learned then that she was a vegetarian.

When I reached Matilde's house I called out her name from the street and she invited me up. She was dozing in the warmth of the hearth as she always did when she was not busy looking after her animals or going here and there during the hours when the winter sun still gave off a little heat. Like a cat, she had her own territory. It was limited on one side by the fountain with its five jets, then by the bakery, which was as high as she went, and lower down her boundaries coincided with the natural limits of the village. Her house was on the east side of the village, close to a path that led her into the country whenever she needed to collect kindling. Alone, bent double, she carried a bundle of dry sticks that she used sparingly to make them last several days. When I went into the kitchen I found her taciturn and in no mood for gossip. Nevertheless, I pointed to a framed photograph hanging on the wall and asked:

'Was that your husband?'

'He was a tyrant,' she answered, confirming with a brief nod of her head.

'How old was he when he died?'

'He was forty-two. I've been a widow ever since. And he was sixteen years older than I. But I didn't want to get married again. I wasn't prepared to put up with another man.'

Matilde fell silent to show her lack of interest, then abruptly, as though wishing to change the subject, she told me she had a bad headache.

'Would you like me to fetch you some aspirin?' I willingly offered.

'No, child, aspirin's no good for this kind of pain.'

I sat down in front of the fire without having been invited. At other times I enjoyed asking her about the objects I saw round the house. I was always amazed to discover that she had a tale for each of them. I can remember, once, pointing to a winding frame lying on a small table with a half-wound ball of wool, as though she were using it. I said: 'Do you like knitting?'

'I don't see well enough for that sort of thing now,' she answered, and went on to tell me that she never touched the winding frame; she had left it there, just where it was at the death of the aunt to whom it had belonged, as had also the house that Matilde had inherited and now lived in. She also told me that previously her aunt and uncle had owned a better house but their life had been made impossible because of the 'Fears' that lived in it.

'The Fears are the souls of the dead,' she explained. There were so many of them that they couldn't sleep at night. And even the Martinicos, who are invisible spirits that everyone seems to know in this country, lived in fear. At last they decided to move. They were hardly settled in the new house when her aunt complained that she had forgotten the winding frame. A bodyless voice behind her hastened to assure her that they had seen to bringing it over. It was a Martinico. They had all followed the masters of the house. It was evident that neither the humans nor the Martinicos would ever escape from the souls. For the Fears had moved house too. She concluded by saying: 'And they're all here still. They don't worry me. But sometimes. . . . What an uproar!'

Matilde spoke of these things quite naturally. The Fears and the Martinicos were more or less as real to her as the winding frame, her aunt and uncle and even the house itself.

'Why don't you splash some cold water on your face?' I suggested, as she let out a slight moan of pain in the silence where we sat.

'Mercy, child! Don't talk to me about water, either hot or cold. At my age it can't be healthy' – and she let out a sigh of resignation as she spoke.

I realized that she intended to put up with the pain without doing anything to alleviate it. And also that she did not understand my concern. She looked at me in astonishment every time I suggested a remedy. Her suffering seemed to have no

importance, none at all. With her eyes half
closed and a strained expression on her face,
forgetting her own suffering as she proceeded,
she began telling me how in the 'old days' there
really had been sickness and horror but, luckily,
they had gone for ever. She had still not forgotten
the epidemics which in her youth had devastated
whole villages at a time. When the cholera epidemic began she was eighteen years old. Sometimes, without anything happening to bring it to
mind, she would remember scenes from that
time. On one occasion she had gone to the pest-
house set up outside the village somewhat higher
than the first house, and seen a man trying to
push a corpse into one of the tombs that had
already been dug in the ground. And she had also
seen how the corpse, who wasn't dead but only
seemed to be, waved his weak arms from the
hole, trying to grasp the feet of the grave-digger.
That scene, glimpsed through a cloud of dust
raised by the grave-digger's shovel as he tried to
quieten the supposed corpse, seemed a nightmare
and a lie. But she knew at once that it wasn't, that
the authorities had decided to bury the dying at
the first signs of faintness or loss of conscious-
ness. They were convinced that if the infected

people died underground the epidemic would subside. Later on, death by cholera became a little less merciless: the sick were simply taken to the cemetery and there, accompanied by their families, they died next to the grave that had been prepared for them. Some, very few, managed not to die, to get well and return to their homes.

Matilde recounted these calamities absorbed and lost in a time that had terrified her and did not seem to have left her entirely. It was a crystallized 'before' that still formed part of the present. A 'before' where they had only one comb and only one broom for a whole street, where, because of the money they had been forced to borrow, every peasant and every shepherd was irredeemably in debt to the few rich men who lived in the village. These debts could never be written off, not even with their own wives and daughters, not with all the time between sunrise and sunset, not with their whole lives.

Matilde prided herself on the independence she had achieved with no help from anyone. She received a miserable widow's pension that arrived irregularly. But she had succeeded in surviving alone thanks to her few animals, but above all, as she used to say with satisfaction, because from a very early age she had learned to keep herself alive on practically nothing. Before I left, and in spite of the headache that tormented her and which she considered incurable and unpredictable, she still had heart enough to tell me how she had met Elsa, for it was precisely because of a headache that they had come to meet.

She saw her for the first time sitting on the doorstep of a house close to hers. It was a good place from which to sit in contemplation of the mountains that could be seen outlined against the horizon on clear days. It would not have surprised Matilde to see a stranger at the foot of the house, had the stranger been occupied in admiring the view. But this was not the case: Elsa had buried her head in her arms, resting them on her knees. At first Matilde thought that she was crying. But on approaching her to offer assistance, should it be needed, she recognized the signs of a different kind of suffering on her face. When she heard that the whole left side of her head was atrociously painful, she had a feeling of kinship, as she too suffered frequently from the same complaint. She invited Elsa into her house intending to give her some aspirin. Elsa looked at her resentfully, but nonetheless gratefully accepted her offer. Matilde said that from the very first, Elsa had struck her as a very fragile helpless person and she had immediately felt a desire to protect her. She added that even then she guessed that something very serious was happening to her.

I took leave of Matilde, leaving her in the shelter of her kitchen and the warmth of her fire, patiently waiting for her pain to subside. It was time to visit Elsa, as I did most evenings. I went from one house to the other without any thoughts: my energies went into the unpleasant business of looking out for all the stones. Even now I haven't really got used to these streets; just walking along and looking at the countryside or what was going on around me was unthinkable that evening. I could not concentrate on anything other than my footsteps; the stones that littered the ground made it impossible. I had to go up and down the hills paying great attention to the ground I was walking on and carefully choosing every spot where I put my feet. Not for one moment was I free from the danger of slipping or stumbling, from the constant fear of falling.

On coming into Elsa's house I noticed with pleasure the smell of damp, clean wood, wood enclosed in an uninhabited house. It was a warm, welcoming smell contrasting with my own house where I could never get rid of the chicken-coop smell. Even though I went to great pains to shut doors and windows tightly, supposing it to come from the neighbouring houses, the smell of hens and rabbits remained permanently inside.

10

It was getting late and I found Elsa closing the windows. As soon as night fell she would hasten impatiently to shut all the shutters as though she were afraid of being watched by faceless eyes hidden in the dark behind the window panes. More than once she had been startled in the night, hearing light sounds, careful as the footsteps of a cat. And frequently it was indeed cats that wandered into the house if by the slightest oversight a door or a window had been left ajar.

Elsa had taken an important step in her relationship with Agustín Valdés. She had phoned him. She was full of enthusiasm at the way he had responded to her. They had had a long conversation and Agustín's voice was engraved on her memory, stirring up extraordinary exaltation and sensuality. She had discovered strong affinities between them. She was convinced that never in her life had she reached a degree of communication so intense as she had with him. She had

finally decided to give him her address and her
phone number. This opened her to the uncertainties of expectation; and even if such expectation was justified, it was nonetheless fraught with
fear and anxiety. Every afternoon straight after
lunch she would go and sit on the terrace. And
then the tea or coffee she took, the book she read,
the patient waiting and, later, the watching of the
red bus climbing slowly like a tortoise, zigzag-
ging along the road, disappearing and reappearing as it ascended through the mountains to the
village, all this would become part of a daily ritual fed by her passion. Thus her afternoons passed, one after the other, ruled by an inordinate
hope that rested entirely on a letter from Agustín
Valdés, a letter which might not even come in the
red bus carrying the day's mail.

As soon as I entered the house and greeted her
I was aware that she had undergone a transforma-
tion: her movements had become quicker and
more vital, she smiled with her eyes, with her
lips, with her whole body. An aura of happiness
radiated from her and lit up everything that surrounded her. Her excited voice was pitched
higher than usual and she hurried on nervously
trying to describe what she had felt when at long

last, that very afternoon, she had received the much-desired letter. She insisted on showing it me. I read it with a certain feeling of embarrassment and did not find in it sufficient justification for so much enthusiasm. I thought it sincere and friendly, but she had concentrated on one single sentence, I now think perhaps rightly. It said: 'Phone me sometimes, even if I never phone you (and don't hold it against me – in exchange I promise to write to you, as it is when I write that my heart is united with the atmosphere). Love, Agustín.' From the moment of that explicit promise her anxiety increased dangerously. From that day on, like a lookout in a watch tower, she waited on the terrace till she saw the postman coming down the street and going past her door, or, if he did not even come down her street, until she tired of waiting for him. That was her most bitter moment. But despite the sudden loss of heart, she would immediately, anxiously, exert all her energy so as to wrap herself in a multitude of everyday activities: lighting the fire, doing her shopping, tidying the house, making supper, washing clothes. Thanks to these occupations she would contrive to make time pass as quickly as possible so as to arrive at the

next day and with it live again the disproportion-
ate hope she had placed in a single letter. In spite
of this, before going to sleep she would spend
hours lost in her amorous dreaming. It was then
that she wrote her letters to Agustín Valdés and
the entries in the notebook I now have. The fantasy that she was building was solidly grounded in
a musical field, in the melodies she selected,
which – as I have already said – created the
atmosphere necessary for her love, an atmosphere that reached its summit precisely in the
intemporality of music and of night. She said it
was then that, mysteriously, she felt an intimacy
and a closeness that, perhaps, even his actual
presence could not have achieved. She was nearly
able to feel his breath, the warmth of his body,
his loving attention. She wrote in her notebook:

Last night I dreamed of you again, Agustín!
Dream? I am not sure that I can thus name
the places, objects, scenery, people, words
and happenings that appear to me and build
up this other life that I share with you, I do
not know where or when, but which belongs
to me as much as my daily life. I dreamed
that I entered a medium-sized concert hall.

The audience and the orchestra were waiting for me. I was going to give a concert. From the doorway I had already recognized you amongst all the others and felt the warmth of your love surrounding me. I also noticed the tense silence and the unhealthy curiosity the rest of the audience felt about me. I had just come back from some far away place and this was the first concert I was giving since my return. A reproach, bordering on rejection, floated in the atmosphere of the hall. But at the same time I knew that they admired and respected me. I also know that both these contradictory sentiments had been aroused by our love, known to everyone but still a secret that nobody dared mention in your presence or mine. I have not yet found out why this interdiction hung over us, but it was evident that our relationship, which was already of long standing, was illicit.

I remember that on going into the hall I felt both rejected and defiant. In the dream there were a lot of precise allusions to something that had happened that I did not succeed in elucidating. I did not have a particular event present in my mind but I was seething with

the vague unpleasant impressions that a
disagreeable occurrence can leave at the
moment when it is permanently relegated to
memory. These impressions and those I
received from outside seemed to form part of
the net that life weaves around each person.
What I was seeing, surely, was certain hours
in a human life, hours linked to a past and
tending towards a future, with all the hopes,
worries, fears and uncertainties that flow
between one person and others. Those
people, that love, that conflict, including
you, were part of the warp of a life that is
foreign to me, but which nonetheless I
remember as though it were mine. Before
sitting down at the piano I announced firmly
that I would play Mozart's piano concerto
number twenty-seven. I can remember that
clearly. Then a feeling of vertigo submerged
me. I had just realized that I did not know
how to play any musical instrument
whatever. I could not understand my
rashness, but nevertheless prepared myself to
fulfil mechanically what everyone was
expecting of me. At first the keys did not
exist, they were make-believe, they were

painted on a rigid sheet of metal. In spite of this, I approached my hands hesitantly to the keyboard and suddenly, inexplicably, as if beyond my control, as though flying over the now genuine keys, they started playing a melody that still vibrates in my memory, submerging me in a great wave of plenitude. I really was playing a piano concerto by Mozart. That music was too real to exist only in a dream.

When I finished playing, the applause I received was sparse and polite. I was still seated, closing my eyes, attempting to guess how you were looking at me in those moments. Finally I rose, took a few steps towards the audience; you were amongst them showing me from afar your loving enthusiasm. I acknowledged the applause with a slight bow, which was destined for you alone, as my playing had been. I had played only for you to hear me, the concerto was one of your favourite pieces. I left the podium shortly after, accompanied by two friends whom I cannot identify with anyone I know in real life. You were walking behind me, close to a woman quite a lot older than

I who, in some way, separated us. We were walking slowly and I could feel you a few yards away. I could feel your gaze and your thoughts concentrated on me. During that long walk I existed in silence only for you.

II

Matilde arrived at Elsa's house visibly upset but trying to deceive us with a show of gaiety. That same afternoon she had bought her niche. She didn't like graves, she was terrified at the idea of reposing under the earth and finally mingling with it. She preferred a neat hole in the wall; it would need less looking after and she had no one she could count on to take care of her in the cemetery. Elsa and I tried to share her cheerfulness, all three of us concealing the real meaning of such a purchase. We talked about it without enthusiasm, but tried to demonstrate how satisfactory the acquisition was, as though what really mattered was having purchased a niche at a good price and, what's more, a niche that would be away from the damp thanks to its situation in the sunniest wall of the cemetery. 'I'll be scaring more than one of them,' said Matilde, joking about her own death. Elsa had laughed, forgetting the reason that had brought us together that night in her house. As

soon as she had received Agustín Valdés's letter
she had spent her time rereading it again and
again, writing to him, telephoning him. She anxiously awaited our next hypnotic session. This
time it was I who had fixed the date for the following Friday. I needed to have enough time,
without hurrying, without having to get up early
the following morning. She did not mind Matilde
being present and had therefore invited her to
share in our experiment. I, on the contrary, knew
that I was incapable of putting myself in the right
frame of mind if I had her as a spectator. Matilde
had arrived fully intending to make the evening a
social event, regardless of what it was about. But
her unconcerned, even incredulous attitude to
hypnosis, her foreseeable interruptions, her
unsuitable questions, would act for me as a real
barrier that would make it impossible for me to
play my part. Perhaps the thing that we called
hypnosis contained an element of play-acting,
more or less conscious, but to me it was quite
clear that there was no room for a larger audience
than Elsa and me. Our experiment, already so
fragile, would not bear Matilde's sceptical gaze.
After the purchase which, given her advanced
age, she had felt obliged to make, it did not seem

the right moment to ask her to leave as I intended
to do as soon as an opportunity presented itself. I
could have asked her, apologizing beforehand, to
leave us alone. I could have tried to make her
understand why her presence inhibited me and
promised that later on, when I had mastered the
technique of hypnosis, she could be present at
our sessions. But I felt so embarrassed at asking
her to leave the house, whatever words I might
use, that all I managed to say was: 'Matilde,
please, I have to be alone with Elsa. If you don't
mind, leave now as it's getting late' – and, moreover, I said it with unintentional harshness.

It goes without saying that one cannot talk to
anyone like that without hesitating, using the
warmest tone of voice possible, begging their par-
don repeatedly. Mastering her first disconcerted
reaction she rose, disconsolate and openly
resentful. As she reached the door she turned
round suddenly, with a quietness that amazed
me, gave Elsa a cold look as though insisting at
the last moment that she defend her and take her
side. But Elsa merely promised her that next day
she would tell her what we had discovered in the
experiment. At last Matilde said a sad 'goodnight'
and left with the air of a little girl who has just

been punished. I did not attach much importance to what had just happened and thought that she would soon forget. I was wrong. That impertinence I had allowed myself with Matilde clouded our relationship for ever. From then on she always managed, by some means or other, to keep it present every time we met.

At the time I thought only about Elsa's other story and the story of her dreams which seemed not to be happening in this world and into which my curiosity had already dipped without being able to retreat. Reaching it was so intricate that I could not allow any distraction. I was determined to eliminate any obstacle. Sometimes I think that the attraction and originality of the story whose threads Elsa and I were pulling together lay, as much as anything, in the strange manner in which it appeared to us bit by bit. Even now I am not convinced that the ritual to which we were both devoting ourselves, and which opened the door into that other life in which Elsa assured me she was participating, really was a hypnotic session. But it was quite evident that to reach it we were were obliged to go through with this ceremony. As we listened to Mozart's twenty-seventh piano concerto I swung the diamond ring in front of Elsa's face and she concentrated on its pendulum movement till the tears came to her eyes. As soon as she closed her eyes I devised a test to make sure that she really was sunk in a trance. I realized at once, with excitement, that the door had opened for us, and through it the story we had conjured up duly appeared. Elsa had once again entered the concert hall of her dreams.

'You are playing the piano,' I suggested. 'You are playing a Mozart concerto – number twenty-seven. The audience is listening to you in silence. Agustín is among them, he is looking at you with emotion.'

I did not know whether my words had reached her or not, but even so, when the Mozart concerto came to an end I went on, breaking into the overwhelming silence.

'You have just finished playing. Now you have risen and taken a few steps towards the audience, leaving the piano. Everyone applauds, albeit not very warmly. You are looking at Agustín Valdés. He alone exists for you in these moments. Can you see him? How is he dressed?'

'He's wearing a dark green coat and underneath a white shirt with ruffles, or a bow tied at the neck. I can't quite make out – the hall is in semi-darkness.'

'Who is sitting next to him?'

'There are other people who have already risen to leave. I see them dimly but they seem familiar. He remains seated. He looks at me intently.'

'Look more carefully at the people next to him who have risen. Do you recognize anyone?'

'Yes. Eduardo is standing up too.'

'Eduardo is Agustín?'

'He's walking towards a group of people gathered at the end of the hall. It consists entirely of men. They are his friends. They are talking very softly. I can't hear them.'

'How many people in the group?'

'Now I'm joining them. I'm next to Eduardo, he touches my hand in a barely perceptible caress.'

'How many are there?' I insist.

'Six or seven. I know them all. I have assisted at several meetings with Eduardo.'

'What sort of meetings?'

After a long silence Elsa continued:

'I don't belong to the group, but Eduardo takes me with him occasionally. I'm always on the outside. I don't really understand what they are talking about. There's a complicity between them that they don't share with me. In my presence they talk in veiled terms, intentionally hiding something. Eduardo gets cross if I ask any questions.'

'And now can you hear what they're saying?'

'Now they are silent. They greet one of their number approaching from the other end of the hall. I'm sure he's one of the group because I know him. He's a friend of mine. When he arrives he smiles at me and greets me before the others. Now I'm giving a book to Eduardo – it's not exactly a book, it's a small manuscript amateurishly bound. Eduardo takes it with a worried look. He opens it and starts reading. I too can see it, it's hand-written. The letters are beautifully formed but very hard to read.'

'Try and read something.'

'I can't. But I know that the author is unknown, or rather, it was written by several authors who don't know each other.'

'Why has it been given to Agustín?'

'Agustín was expecting it. Now he's skipping lines, turning pages over as though looking for something. I think he has to write it over again, but in a different way. The friend who brought it to him has joined the group and is talking to the others. His hair is white though he isn't old. His eyes always seem to smile even when he's serious. He has dark circles under his eyes. Now Eduardo has taken my arm, but he immediately leaves me. He greets a woman who has just arrived. She is quite a lot older than I, she must be around forty-five, Eduardo's age. She is very beautiful. Her hair and her clothes are extremely elegant. She smiles coldly at me and congratulates me politely on my performance. I feel annihilated. I am not able to answer her. She turns to Eduardo and both ignore me. She reproaches him for something. I do not know what. She does not speak clearly. I look at Eduardo sadly, his face is tense at first, then gradually takes on an expression of considerable displeasure. He is very angry. She raises the tone of her voice, she is angry too. He turns towards me and looks at me briefly: 'You needn't be afraid.' He says it so lovingly that I tremble. He continues his conversation with the woman.'

'What are they talking about? Listen carefully,' I ordered impatiently, as though she were submerged in a well seeing pictures that I could only hear.

'Bismarck. They are talking about Bismarck,' she answered in a worried voice. 'There is a war. Eduardo is in danger. He's being pursued for something, I don't know what. She's trying to persuade him to flee. She tells him that she has prepared everything necessary for his departure. Now she is saying in a loud voice that she will not allow anything or anyone to detain him in the city. She gives me a long cruel look. She goes away without taking leave. Eduardo is absorbed in his thoughts. He ignores me. I do not know what is happening to him. Now I can see nothing. Everything has gone black.'

Elsa was silent as though she really were surrounded by intense darkness. Suddenly, without waiting for my questions, she started talking: 'The room is empty, the walls are panelled. I approach a window. The view I can see through it is very familiar, as is the feel of the curtains. They're made of green velvet, they smell dusty.'

After a few moments in which she seemed to have been abandoned by her vision she continued in an anxious voice:

'I'm in a garden. The light is very clear, there are no shadows. Dawn is breaking. I feel cold. Suddenly I see Eduardo in the distance. He is walking very fast. I call him but he does not hear me. I run towards him breathless. He looks at me but does not stop. He goes through a gateway with marble pillars covered in creepers. I catch up with him there. I scream his name. I cannot bear his irritated, distant look. Automatically I lower my eyes to the ground. He stands in front of me without moving, he doesn't speak, he makes no move to come closer. In his right hand he carries a writing case. I recognize it. He keeps his manuscripts in it. Now I remember, he is writing a book. He's wearing a long dark overcoat, his face is half covered by a white scarf. I don't say anything either. I am incapable of speaking. I start crying desperately, I can't control myself. A horse-drawn coach drives up on a nearby track. Eduardo runs towards it, without saying goodbye, without saying a single word. He's abandoning me. He does not even turn his head to look at me when someone from the inside opens the door for him. I watch him get in and disappear.'

Elsa's eyes were shut but she was not asleep, her expression was watchful. This time the silence was longer. I thought I should wake her up and end the session, but she went on:

'The beach is deserted and it's very cold. On the sand close to me there are sheets of iron covered in rust, they are full of holes. I have the presentiment of something horrible . . . an unbearable pain . . . I can see nothing . . . all the pictures have gone. . . . Now Eduardo arrives. He has aged a lot; his dishevelled hair has turned white, his cheeks are very thin, his eyes move restlessly from side to side with an unpleasant expression. This is madness. That is exactly what he looks like: a madman. He rests his hands on the white balustrade that is in front of him. From there he contemplates a beach where the scattered remains of wrecked ships can be seen. That is where I died. I know it. And that is why he gazes at the scene every day. My death was horrible. He knows what it was but I cannot remember anything. I only have vague, distant memories that horrify me.'

Elsa spoke in a low voice, nearly inaudible. At last her vision faded and she slumped in total lassitude. I waited a few minutes before starting to count to ten. When I clapped my hands, which was the signal that brought her back to this world, she opened her eyes and remained very quiet, staring at the fire, showing no interest at all in the scenes she had described aloud, scenes which at her request I had written down in detail. She pushed aside the sheets of paper that I handed her, saying she did not need to read anything as she could remember with precision everything she had seen. She asked me drily to leave her alone, she was very tired and needed silence and sleep. So I left, leaving her prisoner of those visions that, evidently, she was incorporating into herself as though they were deep memories, as though they constituted a past that belonged to her.

12

As soon as I reached my house I wrote down for the second time, and with great care, the notes I had taken during the hypnotic session. I added them to whatever Elsa had said on the previous session and the dreams she had described. I read it all back with a certain enthusiasm, for the story it outlined was acquiring consistency, becoming visible, and its pieces, as in a puzzle, were beginning to come together to form a definite pattern: Southern Germany . . . war . . . 1864 . . . Bismarck. These four pieces already gave shape to a historical moment, for, after a little research, I discovered that Bismarck had in fact been prime minister of Germany for a period stretching from 1862 to 1871. In order to unify a nation he had submitted the country to repeated cruel wars, namely with France, in which the southern part was particularly involved. And that was where, in her hypnotic trance, Elsa had situated the town where the story that was pursuing her had taken place. I endeavoured to avoid the questions that beset me concerning the nature of such a story. All I wanted was to reconstitute it. I had determined to disinter it, to bring it to light in its entirety. And though I was tempted by an irredeemable curiosity, when I asked myself about the darkness from which the story kept emerging, I was snared in threads that always finished by leading me to something I could only think of as an absurdity. On occasion I would try to put some order into the confusion that overcame me, using common sense and a sane outlook. I thought then that Elsa's imagination, transfigured in the hypnotic trance and guided by my questions, acquired the capacity to join together facts, persons, places and events that were already interwoven in her subconscious, so to speak. Elsa had a degree in Philosophy and Literature. She must therefore have studied the history of Germany. I would sometimes arbitrarily decide that Elsa's imagination and memory could come together, even fuse in a game of complicity, to fabricate a story that most likely had no existence other than in her words. I had frequently noticed how her eyes wandered dreamily, suddenly resting on some object, which, I was sure, she did not see. And her attention would remain concentrated on her vision, as though she remembered, as though she returned to the plane of an immense memory that overflowed, extending well beyond the reaches of her past. For in those moments I had the feeling that her imagination became memory and her inventions were converted into events of her own past.

I was so absorbed in the story, in Elsa and her excesses, in the unfolding of her love, that I was suddenly surprised by the nearness of the holidays. The few term days that remained were taken up correcting examination papers and preparing my journey, for I had decided to spend Christmas in Madrid. I saw Elsa only once, when I went to say goodbye. I was not surprised that she did not wish to leave the village, and that the idea of going to town, even for a few days, was unbearable to her. I thought then that she had taken refuge in these mountains amongst people who were nearly non-existent, concealing herself in the unreality of her love, so as to flee a world that frightened her. Nonetheless, days later, in Madrid – feeling lost in the turmoil of the streets, under scraps of dusty sky, grey and dirty, surrounded by a multitude of inexpressive faces and vacant looks; cars on the streets, on the pavement, on the grass of the parks, in doorways, the constant smell of petrol fumes everywhere; going through the tunnels of the underground, meeting old women selling tobacco, whose poverty was so different from that of those other old women in the village – I thought to myself that all that immensity that surrounded me, so complex and noisy, was not much more real than what Elsa was living up there in the mountains, away from the world.

When, two weeks later, I returned to the Alpujarras it seemed to me that the whole village had grown older, as though its streets, its façades and its stones had stored up a little more time. I felt that I was nowhere, that what I was seeing was only a memory. My head was heavy, my ears buzzed and my legs felt like lead when I walked. It took me several days to readapt to the altitude and it was not till then that I went to visit Elsa. It was the hour when the postman usually did his rounds so I imagined her seated on the terrace of her house waiting for a letter from Agustín Valdés. Would she have received it yet, I asked myself as I knocked at her door and realized that the house was empty. During those days Elsa had written in her journal:

. . . When I returned, the shadow of a night
bird flew across the front of my house. I
went in, restless and fleeing from dark birds.
Inside I found only silence. No letter from
you anywhere. Now, at least, I have decided
not to wait any longer. I go off very early in
the afternoon and come back after nightfall,
to forget the postman who rarely comes
down my street, and when he does, passes
my door without stopping. I am already
accepting that you will never write to me,
that I may never see you. Rather as though
you did not exist, as though you never had
existed. I want to think that I am not the
one who loves you, who thinks of you
obsessively, not the one who is destroying
me and overruling me to lead me to despair;
I am not the one who waits for you, who
dreams of you, who, already, is nearly
nothing but you. I am not the one who gives
me a longing for death, and who feels that
anything that is not living with you this love
that I dream, is destruction, damnation and
darkness. That is why I must deny you inside
and outside me; be stronger against those
dreams of love that betray me so many

nights. I manage to get through the
afternoons in the mountains, always alone,
in the most beautiful places, between leafy
trees and streams of transparent water. I flee
from you, but you are everywhere. And now
I know that there is not one single corner in
this world where I could hide myself from
your shadow which saddens me so much.
I would like not even to write to you, but as
you see, it is not possible. Once again, I
realize with despair that my love is not
allowed any other means of fulfilment than
that of being written down
for you.

I like to listen to things that are always
the same, that never change, like the sound
of the wind or the silence of the mountains.
If only I could seek nothing . . . desire
nothing. . . . Death threatens me on all
sides. What a scandal it is to grow old and
die. The sound of the wind carries me far
away, helps me to rest, as it did when I was a
child. Perhaps not even the One God has
power enough to bring you near to me. Or
perhaps only his indifference prevents him.
The world seems to be the same everywhere,

but it is not so. For here, in this village
ignored by history and far from those who
rule the destinies of man, I seem to have
fallen into another world, enigmatic and
cruel. Days here are like the pages of a
book. I feel that I am already touching the
end with one hand. I am too weak and my
despair is too strong for the solitude of the
mountains. I feel that I am poised on a
strange airy platform, launched already
towards death. And you, Agustín, are
destroying me. See how I sicken because
of you: weak because of you, demented
because of you, who only give me silence.
But I have learned to hear your voice
without your talking to me, and that is the
worst. For now I know that your silence is
not silence, nor you indifference,
indifference. Or perhaps it is only my
absurd hope that makes me invent a
fantasy: you – feeling the way I desire you
to feel.

While I waited at Elsa's door, calling occasionally in case she were inside and had not heard
my knocking, or looking around in hope of

seeing her, I discovered Matilde coming down the street to visit her.

'Elsa's not in?' she asked drily, to show that she had not forgiven me.

'I don't think so,' I answered, and at once tried to make excuses for my previous behaviour, evidently at the wrong moment and in the wrong circumstances. I explained as warmly as I could, the reasons that had impelled me to ask her to leave Elsa's house that evening. I said that her presence, or that of anyone, inhibited me and stopped me from concentrating. I added that plunging anyone in a hypnotic trance required – at least in my case – complete isolation.

She listened to me, frowning her mistrust, and when I finished all she said was: 'Yes, of course. And because of "because" you threw me out of the house.'

I realized that my explanations were quite useless. She was concerned only with the fact. The motives that might have led me to such an impertinence were only vague excuses that were not sufficient to mediate between us, even less to reconcile her with me.

'Very well,' I said, discouraged. 'I'm sorry. I'm really sorry.'

I took leave of her with all the friendliness I could muster. I preferred to see Elsa at some other time when Matilde was not there. But next day when I went to visit her, Matilde had already arrived. It seemed to me that Elsa paid no attention to her but simply allowed her to stay, sitting in front of the fire dozing as though she were a cat. As I went in, Elsa greeted me with seeming cheerfulness, but immediately sank into a taciturn silence, punctuated by occasional questions about my journey. I found her somewhat changed. Her cheeks reddened, even burned, by the sun and the heat of the fire, gave her an appearance of health that her eyes, faded by sadness, her slow, weak voice, and her tired gestures, belied at every moment.

It was around that time that she started suffering badly from insomnia and lost her appetite. But in spite of her discouragement, any trivial occurrence external to her thoughts, in which she could read an allusion to her love, sufficed for her hope to be revived again. I found her one day radiating happiness that I could only attribute to the arrival of a letter from Agustín Valdés or something similar. She was sitting on the terrace and saw me while I was still a good way from

her house. The sun had not yet set behind the
Tajo Gallego and it was cold, but she lingered on,
a book in her hand, reading and rereading a passage that, she said, she had only just come across.
What had most impressed her in the message that
had just sprung from the pages of Proust's *The
Fugitive* was, precisely, the manner in which it
had come to her. If she had discovered it whilst
reading normally, she would not have been so
moved. But the discovery had been different:
she'd been sitting on the terrace, proposing once
again to wait for the day's mail. While she
poured herself a cup of tea she had left the book
lying in her lap. An involuntary movement had
opened it, and as she'd brought the cup to her lips
she had glanced casually at some lines. They
read:

And moreover, in the history of a love and
its battles against oblivion, do not dreams
occupy a space greater even than waking? At
night, sleep arranges a meeting for us with
the one whom we would finish by forgetting
– if only we never saw her again. For, say
what you will, we may well be convinced
that what is happening to us in dreams is real.

Out of the enthusiasm stirred up by these words, came another letter to Agustín Valdés. This time she sent him a photograph of herself on which she appeared with a supernatural beauty and harmony of features hard to find in a human face. She enclosed a note that said: 'Allow me at least to introduce a likeness of myself into your house since I cannot into your soul. For I fear that you never remember me and would not even recognize me should you see me. My greatest desire is to live in your solitude, your nights, your sleep, your dreams – just as you have lived in me for so long a time.

13

Elsa had closed her eyes sooner than on previous occasions. I stopped the pendulum movement of the diamond ring and by the light of a single candle I concentrated on suggesting to her a scene and a situation that she herself had outlined a few minutes before, when recounting the latest dream in which Agustín Valdés had appeared. In spite of this she took a long time to answer. Minutes were passing and I repeated my questions and suggestions insistently; but, sunk deeply in some remote place, she gave no sign of having heard me. Her expressionless face was relaxed in deep repose. Uncertain of what to do I tried to guess what pictures were appearing to her from the darkness in which she seemed submerged.

Once again, standing in front of her, I described in a loud voice the scene of her latest dream: 'You are in a house in the country, in a small, very light room with big windows. You are standing near a window, and outside, on the window ledge, there are pots with flowering plants. There is a garden too, and further on a leafy grove. Can you describe the inside of the room?'

'Eduardo is in front of me,' she at last replied with the same ease as previously. 'He is reading some sheets of paper. I think it's a letter. He is furious. Now he's shouting angrily. Everything seems to tremble at his voice.'

'Eduardo is Agustín?'

'Yes,' she said briefly, answering at last a question she did not seem to have heard on previous occasions.

'Why is he shouting like that?' I asked. 'Because of what he's reading? Is he cross with you?'

'Not with me. It's the letter that makes him furious.'

'Can you hear what he's saying?'

'There's a war. He's talking about political problems and people I don't know.'

'And you're not saying anything?'

'I'm trying to calm him. But I make it worse. He gets even angrier.'

'What's happening now?'

'Nothing. I'm looking at him. I love him

intensely. I feel so much love in those moments . . ..'

'Can you describe the room you're in?'

'I stand up and leave. It's night. I'm alone. I'm frightened. It's very cold.'

'Where are you going?'

'I'm very tired. I'm rowing in a small boat. I'm alone. It's night. I can smell stagnant water. I'm rowing along the shore. The branches of the trees scratch my face, I push them aside with one hand. The leaves are wet and slippery. There are a lot of mosquitoes. I try to get rid of them by shaking my head, but it's useless. I keep on rowing, my hands are sore.'

'Why are you alone?'

'I'm coming back alone. I've left Eduardo on the other side.'

'Where is he going?'

'He's gone to join the others.'

'Who are the others?'

'They are his friends.'

'What are they going to do?'

'He hasn't told me anything. Now I can hear a dreadful scream. I can't recognize the voice. I'm afraid it might be Eduardo. I turn the boat round and go in the opposite direction. I hardly have enough strength left to go on rowing. I want to go back to the other shore. In the middle of the lake I hear that dreadful scream again. I call Eduardo. No one answers. I dip the oars in the water and keep on. The boat seems not to move in spite of my efforts. The other bank stays as far away as ever. Now I can see it, muddy and dark, wrapped in an aura of menace. I'm frightened but I can't abandon Eduardo; I must know what has happened to him. There's nobody. I don't know which way to go. I can hardly see anything. The ground is soggy and my feet sink heavily into the mud. I'm lost. . . . Now I can see the lake again: an enormous flat expanse, black and shining. I can hear it murmur at each stroke of the oars. I'm moving very slowly . . . very slowly.'

'Did you find Eduardo?' I asked.

'No. But I didn't want to go back without knowing what had happened.'

'Why did you leave without having seen him?'

'I don't know. I think they were pursuing me.'

'You have left the boat on the shore. You are looking for Eduardo. What happens?'

'I can see a man standing up on a wall, very close to me. I think it is Eduardo. But he jumps down on me and holds me tightly by the arms. I scream, terrified. It's not Eduardo. I've never seen this man. He laughs like a madman. . . . I manage to free myself and run away. He comes after me, he's shouting at me. He wants to know where Eduardo is. He's furious. He stops by some hawthorn bushes. I can't hear him any longer. I look back; his clothes seem to have been caught in the hawthorn bushes. He tries to free himself. I go on running. My only thought is to reach the boat and escape. I know there's only one, so he won't be able to follow me across the lake.'

'Did you meet him again?'

'Yes. When I get to the other side three men are waiting for me. I know at once that they are with him. The three of them are waiting very quietly. They know that this time I can't run away. Now I can see a cement floor and peeling, dirty walls. I'm sitting on the floor. Close to me there is a puddle of water. Everything is in semi-darkness. There's a strong smell of damp and alcohol. I can see military boots all around me. I can't see the faces of the men who are wearing them. I can't look up. I'm lying on the floor and my body feels very heavy. I can't even move. I don't know what is happening to me. I hear that man's voice and listen again to his madman's laugh. He questions me intently about Eduardo. He wants to know where he is. I hear his voice from very far off. He's yelling at me but I don't feel concerned. I can't talk, I am surrounded by military boots moving impatiently and violently. I feel an unbearable terror.'

'What do these men say to you? Do they ask you anything else?'

'I don't know. I can't see anything. . . . Now I seem to hear the murmur of the waves on the seashore. I can feel damp sand under my body. They have brought me here, very far from my home. I am lost. There is no one near me. I can see fragments of metal with remains of paint and bits of rusty iron I can't identify. My left hand clutches a bar of rusty iron, my fingers feel it, rough and cold. I don't know what's happening.'

Elsa was silent, an expression of anguish fixed on her face. I noticed that her lips were moving as though she were articulating inaudible words, as though her voice were sounding in some place inaccessible to me.

'Out loud, please! Louder,' I insisted anxiously, feeling intuitively at the same time that it wasn't a matter of talking louder. I wanted to go on listening to those visions that I could not see.

Finally I opted for trusting to her memory, for she always remembered on waking whatever she had seen in her hypnotic trance – or whatever it might be. As soon as it was possible I tried to bring her back to a state of wakefulness. Afterwards, when I asked her about those scenes that I had not been able to hear, she assured me that she could not remember any scenes other than those she had described out loud.

14

Elsa wandered through the village like a boat adrift, ghost-like, floating past rows of irregular, haphazardly built house fronts arranged up and down the narrow streets like those of a child's toy town. She never looked outwards, neither at the old women who crossed her path, survivors of a way of life now gone; nor at the sheep, nor at the goats with their sleepwalkers' eyes, so nearly human; nor at the children, nor the men, nor the youths; not even at the mountains. Everything that surrounded her had crystallized into dream shadows, which might receive the light of the sun or of the moon – to her it was of no importance. Her time had become other, indifferent to day or night; it became real only in the fiction of her dreams and visions. For that was where she really lived. She no longer phoned Agustín Valdés. She didn't dare. Her great fear was that his voice would be harsh, laconic, or politely amiable. Writing was different. She could imagine or invent the

impressions and emotions her words might gen-
erate in him. She had written to him twice, on
consecutive days. One of her letters read:

If you were not a shadow . . . if I had not
invented you . . . if I had conjured you up
out of dreams and visions risen from strange
depths in me . . . but that cannot be. Yet
you are only a shadow and that is why
I sicken, for shadows cannot die.

In the other letter she had written:

Agustín, I cannot forget you, neither by day
nor by night. And I cannot understand that
the same thing is not happening to you.
I refuse to admit that our meeting was
meaningless, that all these signs, perceptible
only to me, were no more than empty
coincidences. I am frightened by things that
just happen for no reason, arbitrary, blind
things, like those hollow words that some
birds learn to pronounce.

And in her notebook she had written:

I feel quite simply that I am dying. My heart
seems to pause and stay suspended in a

strange heartbeat that floods my whole body
with the most profound horror. The nights
are endless. I am alone, and anything is
possible beneath this timeless darkness. My
hands feel very far from me; my whole body
is now made of air, a metallic humming
batters my head; I am separated from
everything that surrounds me. I try to
reassure myself: 'Don't believe it! Nothing is
happening!' And each time my heart misses a
beat, I asphyxiate. I pray to some god to help
me, but I am alone under an infinite black
pall. I would like to live a little longer; I feel
that something oppresses my breast and that
life is leaving me. I don't know what is
happening to me, but I have the impression
that I am already somewhere else.
My greatest desire at this very moment, is
not to die yet. But I think that I am dead
already to everything except this hope of
love. Agustín, if this love is not possible,
I will not be able to live.

Elsa, caught in what was, in the beginning,
perhaps only a game, had lost control. Now she
was sinking in a mire that overcame her, trapped

in a net that she herself had woven, which she no longer understood. For the first time I was really alarmed and realized how serious her condition was. When there were just the two of us, I tried various approaches to make her think; but during the moments we were together she was not capable of saying or thinking anything. The intensity of her grief, of her despair, of her love, all conjoined, amazed me. Her story was doomed from the beginning. I never discerned in her the slightest interest in the eventual fulfilment of what she was living – whatever that might be. It seemed that her only interest was contemplation, being the spectator of a love story that was supposedly hers; but it was rather as if someone were to try jumping into the water without getting wet. My reaction was so strictly one of common sense that I began to feel uncomfortable. None the less, a time came when I decided to intervene and urge her to go to Barcelona and visit Agustín Valdés. To me it seemed necessary that she come in contact with the reality of a person who existed for her entirely on an imaginary plane.

'I don't know whether I'll go,' she answered. 'Just the idea of meeting someone who isn't him destroys me. What I fear most are those daily gestures, perhaps meaningless, but which are familiar and in which we recognize each other without even realizing it. It's how one puts on an overcoat, fastens a button, drinks coffee, walks in the street, looks at something that has taken one's notice. It occurs to me that in all those gestures one doesn't even notice normally, he's going to appear to me as a stranger. And worst of all will be the way he'll come towards me. How do you think he will treat me? As though we had just met? I can just imagine it.'

'In spite of all that, you must go and see him,' I insisted. 'He's all that too. You've got to take the risk.'

'What intrigues me,' she said, 'is the meaning of the story in which he appears, of those dreams that recur, of all that I see when hypnotized. Where does it all come from?'

'I think you should be asking yourself something different,' I said, playing my role of sensible person. 'Why doesn't he write to you or phone you? Why is he so detached from this story? Why is there no echo in him of all that is happening to you, and only to you?'

'I don't know what's happening to him. And I don't think you do either. But I don't think he is detached from this story, and I'm sure it's not indifference that he feels.'

'Well, if that's so, why don't you go and see him?'

'I don't know. But I may well go. I'll think about it.'

For a week I was hardly able to speak to Elsa – she had no time for anything. She allowed Matilde her constant visits, for Matilde was equal to any role or situation. She could limit herself to looking at Elsa silently from the street door for an indefinite period or sitting beside her warming herself at the hearth, without venturing to utter more than a conventional greeting. Of course, if Elsa allowed her, she would lose herself in long stories about the past. Only very occasionally – the instances could be counted on the fingers of your hand – would she reveal her own opinions, which she usually kept distrustfully to herself. One evening I arrived hoping to find my friend alone, but without success. On another occasion I found Matilde dozing in a rocking chair in front of the fire. She did not even answer my greeting, so I presumed she had not heard me, as I had kept my voice as low as possible, in the hope that she would not notice me and follow me to Elsa's bedroom, as she had done on previous occasions. At last I was able to be alone with my friend. I learned that she had already announced her visit to Agustín Valdés. She had slightly less than a week to prepare herself. She passed her time in front of a high, rectangular looking-glass that she herself had moved into her bedroom, putting on all the clothes she had, trying different combinations, different hairstyles and make-up. It wasn't because she wished to impress him with her beauty. What she sought in her face, in her whole appearance, was that supernatural air that shone out of the only photograph of herself she had ever sent him. She wanted him to recognize her, to be once again that image, recover that long-since crystallized moment, distant and irretrievable. She was in despair at the deep circles round her eyes, at her skin now dull and desperately pale. She hardly ate, not only from lack of appetite but sometimes through indolence, sometimes because she hadn't found time to go up to the shop, buy food and cook it. A haziness, due to her permanent weakness, clouded her mind. She fought it by drinking endless cups of coffee. When she became aware of me, looking at her in silence without venturing into the room, she didn't even greet me. She at once started complaining about how sick she looked and how useless make-up was, as the pallor of her skin always finished by showing under any sort of tinted face cream.

'I don't know why I've got myself into this,' she complained. 'What an idea! Visit him! This meeting could be a catastrophe!'

'It strikes me as the most normal thing you could do.'

'Oh, give over with normal!'

'And if you suit each other,' I stupidly tried to cheer her up, 'you could stay on in Barcelona, see him frequently . . . I don't know, perhaps even live with him. Wouldn't you like that?'

'Oh, that's enough! Live . . . live . . . how mundane you are!'

Quite evidently, visiting Agustín Valdés counted for her not as an important stage in her love story, but rather as a considerable and unnecessary disturbance. She was afraid of not recognizing him, even that she might feel estranged from him.

'Do you know,' she said suddenly, 'I can't even remember how he was dressed. Though I suppose it doesn't really matter, does it?'

'Of course it doesn't,' I agreed, afraid she would lose heart and cancel her trip.

I think that both of us suspected that this meeting might be the end of her strange love story. In spite of this, I lied to her with no feeling of remorse.

'Of course he wants to see you,' I said, 'and get to know you a bit better. He's going to be terribly intrigued.'

'Do you really think so?' she answered, without concealing her anxiety.

During those days I could see clearly the bitterness and desolation that surrounded her love. I was frightened for her. I saw her heading for some desperate end. If any possibility existed of changing the sad course that her fantasy had taken, it was precisely in a confrontation with Agustín Valdés, even at the risk of shattering herself on a reality which, I was quite sure, would never coincide with her dreams.

The night before her departure she came to my house to say goodbye. It seemed to me that she moved, thought, spoke, under the weight of a deep-seated fear. She talked nervously and incoherently. Her visit was short; she had to get up at dawn next morning as the only bus left the village very early. She spent a sleepless night, not even going to bed. Before dawn she came to see me, completely defeated. I was still asleep when I heard her banging on my door.

'I'm not going,' she said briefly, too down-hearted even to greet me or excuse herself for waking me up at such an early hour. 'I can't. I can't. Just as I can't fly. It's the same sort of impossibility. It doesn't depend on me.'
As she said these words she collapsed into an armchair and said nothing more. I tried to make what was happening to her seem unimportant. I assured her that I understood her: of course it was a difficult meeting; perhaps it would be better if she visited him at some other time, when she felt more rested. Suddenly she started crying, silently, as though she had no strength left for more audible sobs. She wept on motionless, not allowing a complaint or a sigh to pass her lips. Only her tears moved, sliding abundantly down her cheeks.

15

In some way, Elsa enjoyed living her upsurge of love passively, without resistance, allowing herself to be surprised by various signs that seemed intended for her, which a strange destiny scattered on her path. They were portents, charged with meaning, that came upon her unexpectedly. She hoarded them and used them to construct irrefutable proofs of a mysterious story, which thus did not originate only in her mind, however unfathomable or unknown it might appear to her. And all around her, signs had been accumulating that affected her dangerously.

When, a few days after cancelling her journey, she phoned Agustín Valdés again, she immediately recovered her spirits. He had been expecting her with real interest and even impatience, she told me. He even showed disappointment at not having been able to see her. They kept up a long, intense conversation in which he advised her insistently to read a book of Goethe's, *Elective Affinities*. She set off for Granada as soon as possible in order to buy the book, and there, in the selfsame shop where she found it, she was surprised by another link in the chain of hints that were invading her along the fragile path of her love. It was a postcard reproduction of a portrait of Goethe contemplating the cut-out silhouette of a woman. It was dated 1778. She had met Agustín Valdés in 1978. But even more important: was this not a portrait of herself? Was she not equally dedicated to contemplation of the shadowy face of an absent love? She framed the postcard with great care and placed it on her bedside table, leaning it against the wall, as though it had been the picture of a saint.

I still don't know exactly when I began to be haunted by the idea of phoning Agustín Valdés myself. I would, of course, do so in my friend's name, with the sole intention of helping her. But I cannot deny that, at the same time, I was urged on by curiosity; I wanted to hear the sound of his voice, to confirm that he really existed, and discover what he would find to say to me. I tried to imagine him through the portrait Elsa had painted with her words. And, so that the phone call, which I finally, furtively put through – more or less stealing the number from my friend's diary – should not appear to me as treachery, I gave myself a solid excuse: I must know something definite about his attitude to Elsa. It was not just an excuse, it was the motive that incited me to look through the loophole that the telephone afforded us, to view a little of the reality of Agustín Valdés. I had to know what his attitude was so as to help Elsa, for it was undeniable that her feelings were already acquiring morbid, even dangerous aspects and I was becoming really alarmed.

When Agustín Valdés answered the phone and I introduced myself as a friend of Elsa's, all he said was, 'Oh yes?' From the very beginning his voice was warm and the tone he used throughout our conversation, and not just in the first monosyllables, was cordial and sincere, even when faced with the information I gave him concerning the state Elsa was in, or when I could not conceal my irritation at his answers.

'The truth is that it never entered my mind that Elsa was suffering,' he said at one moment of our conversation. 'I can't understand it, and moreover I do not feel that those letters were intended for me.'

'Yes. But you encouraged her to write to you and phone you,' I answered.

'I did?'

'Yes, of course. You said in your letter, "Phone me sometimes, even though I don't phone you (and don't hold it against me – in exchange I promise to write to you, for it is when I write that my heart is united with the atmosphere . . .)." You must be surprised that I can repeat that sentence from memory.'

'I wrote that?'

'Surely you haven't forgotten?' I protested.

'Yes, I think I can remember now. And if I wrote her that, it's because I felt it at the time.'

'So?'

'Why don't I write to her? Listen, you've caught me at a very painful moment. I too am very involved in a love story. I am living an *amour fou* with a married woman. It's very difficult. I'm so very much absorbed.'

'Very well. But why not tell her? How can you allow her to go on loving, or whatever it is, without knowing what's happening to you?'

'I don't know. I hadn't thought of it. And moreover, this love of hers – or whatever it is, as you say – seems so productive. . . .'

'Perhaps, but only relatively so. It's doing her a lot of harm.'

'I didn't see it that way. Speak to her if you want to. I don't know what to do. All this leaves me confused.'

I can't remember whether I agreed that I would talk to her, or if I just thought it. I took leave curtly – he could think what he wanted – and, thoroughly irritated, I put down the phone. 'So what, *amour fou*?' I hissed between my teeth as I left the phone booth. 'What a cretin! High-faluting nonsense!' These insults were followed out loud by many others as I walked back to my house. For in truth, the conversation had disappointed me deeply. I felt – perhaps without any valid justification – that the story I had been pursuing through Elsa had suddenly lost its support, its possible connection with reality. It remained floating in the air, lonely, abandoned, unreal. I could not understand why Agustín Valdés had not been fascinated; that Elsa's letters, her voice, her love, had not been for him a siren's song to whose spell he should already have succumbed. The opposite had been true. He had not paid the slightest attention to Elsa. He had stopped his ears with wax: just like Ulysses. Instead, he had let himself be trapped in a tawdry adventure – of its tawdriness I had no doubt – which he had the gall to call '*amour fou*'. As I recalled his smooth voice, I was sure it belonged to someone soft and apathetic, to someone who did not enjoy sufficient drive and imagination to be worthy of a love like Elsa's. Yes – but who was ever going to be worthy of her love? I realized that she was totally alone and that she loved with genuine passion someone who did not exist. I decided to say nothing about my conversation with Agustín Valdés, and from now on to refuse to take part in building her chimera. When, two days after her visit to Granada, she came to visit me, stirred up by her reading of Goethe's *Elective Affinities* and rebelling against the passivity she showed in her own story, I thought it my duty to show her the Agustín Valdés I had encountered in our short conversation. It was urgently necessary to restrain her, especially as she informed me excitedly that she had decided to visit him at last. She seemed miraculously to have overcome her recent inability to meet him on terms of reality. Discovering this novel – especially at his suggestion – had been the most surprising coincidence in her amorous progress, and at the same time the most inexplicable. She started by informing me that the hero bore the name that Agustín was given in her hypnotic trance: Eduardo.

'I wouldn't look for anything significant in that if I were you,' I said casually. 'You must agree that Eduardo is a pretty common name.'

She didn't bother to answer me; she was in too much of a hurry to lay before me all the coincidences she had found in the novel. She spoke excitedly, and from the very beginning did not expect me to understand, for my answers were scornful, though they made no impression on her. She was amazed at the importance the book gave to those coincidences that normally appear nonsensical or insignificant – an importance matched in the story that she herself was living. She told me that on one occasion at the beginning of his love for Otilia, Eduardo, at a banquet, had thrown a glass in the air after drinking from it. It was the custom to break glasses in this fashion as an expression of enjoyment. But on this occasion, not only did the glass not break, but moreover, the letters E and O were found to be engraved on it.

'Don't you find it significant that he plays with coincidences in that way?'

'Well, no. It doesn't convey anything to me,' I answered. 'Also I'd have to read the book to get the meaning of the anecdote.'

'I've also found resemblances between Otilia and me; at least the me that appears in the story. For example, she often used to keep dried flowers. . . .'

'For goodness sake!' I protested, interrupting her deliberately. 'Who hasn't kept dried flowers at some time or other in his life?'

'Also she used to have terrible headaches on the left side, just like me.'

'You're not suggesting that's a rare complaint, are you?'

'And that ghastly state I sometimes get into, when it's absolutely impossible to move or utter a sound. It happened to Otilia twice.'

'All right. That's a curious coincidence, but nothing more.'

'There are lots of others that I'm not going to tell you. But you've got to listen to the most important one of all: the end of the novel. There's a lake and something tragic happens there. From then on Otilia falls into a state that leads to her death. And Eduardo, refusing to accept that she's no longer alive, gives orders that she continue to be served, bringing food and clothes to her room, as though she hadn't died. He does everything he can to stop her from being buried. He goes mad. That doesn't impress you either? Such close similarity to the story unfolding in my dreams and the hypnotic sessions. Why are the two stories so alike? Why did it have to be Agustín Valdés who suggested I read the book when I have never spoken to him of our secret story?'

'Don't get so upset,' I said, putting as sceptical a tone in my voice as I could. 'Be sensible, Elsa. All love stories, whether in novels or films, are more or less the same, especially the unhappy ones, which are the most interesting. There's always death and madness. It's more or less axiomatic. Your imagination, in your dreams as also under hypnosis, has been influenced by a multitude of books, which you can't even remember. That's a possible explanation. And it's no more important than that.'

'Don't be so simple, Maria!' she said, discouraged by my attitude. 'Next time you hypnotize me I want you to question me about the resemblances with *Elective Affinities* I've been telling you about.'

'There won't be a next time,' I said firmly.

'Why not?'

'I don't intend to go on encouraging you in this fantasy. It's interesting if you just take it as a game. But as far as I can see, it's not a game for you. I'm not going to collaborate any longer in this sort of thing. What you need is to meet a real man and have a real story.'

'Don't talk nonsense!' she suddenly shrieked, beside herself. 'I don't want a man! I don't want a man! I only want to feel love the way I'm feeling it now. Regardless of where it comes from!'

As soon as she'd finished she left without a further word, not even pausing to shut the street door. I did not in the least question the veracity of her words. But it was evident to me that she was being pulled two ways and was no longer able to keep even the necessary minimum of balance. She did not want a man. She was not lying when she made such a statement; but at the same time she seemed firmly resolved to visit Agustín Valdés. She was at last conscious of the necessity of walking on solid ground. But in spite of this, in the letter that she wrote him around this time, she did not dare tell him of her decision to visit him.

Dear Agustín,

The days pass, I go from one place to another and you do not change within me. Not for one instant can I forget you. My efforts to concentrate on other things are useless. My head seems possessed by a thick, sweet mist, which you alone inhabit. A diabolical machine has been let loose in it and I cannot stop dreaming of you in a thousand different situations; though I always discover in the end that you are not with me, that it is not even possible for me to see you. When I remember your voice, and it seems I can almost hear it, my whole body trembles. Every morning, when I wake up, it is you I feel, more than myself, who am now become a ghost, a sanctuary for your image. Neither distance, absence, nor time, nor yet the darkness that now covers me, matter. You are always within me. Sometimes I think I could go to Barcelona, live there and see you when you allowed me to. But something stops me. Perhaps the fear of suffering your indifference closer to. Oh, I don't know! But it is as powerful as that other force that draws me towards you.

This dream state is now permanent. I can do

nothing, nor yet can I live. Now I do not even need to move, indeed I hardly can. I shut my eyes and live with you wherever I am, all the time. For you I sicken. I feel I am fallen into a very deep well. Anaemia and weakness leave me nearly lifeless at times, but even then you are still with me. Now I cannot feel anything that is not you. I try to recover my health, but I cannot. For a long time I have lived in constant anxiety. I cannot sleep, nor rest; I can hardly eat. For you I am dying and I am not capable of doing anything to see you. I fear that you will never be able to love me.

If you knew the extent of my despair perhaps you would be more generous with me. But why should you be anything other than what you are, if you hardly know me, if you hardly remember me, if on seeing me you did not feel the way I felt?

Dear Agustín, I cannot give up writing to you, for it is only then that I feel that, in some way, I can rest.

My love, Elsa

16

I t was the middle of the night when Elsa gave my door a violent push, opened it with a bang, and entered my house, emerging from the thick blackness outside. On seeing her I sat up with a jerk. The expression on her face was new to me. It was neither fear, nor sadness, nor worry. It was a broken expression, mute, nameless, composed of features in dissolution. She hesitated slightly, then threw herself into my arms, crying, screaming, gesticulating wildly. I tried to calm her without daring to question her. At last, between sobs, she managed to speak. She had phoned Agustín Valdés to tell him of her visit, confident that he would be delighted with the news. But this time it was not so. He openly refused to see her, said it quite clearly, not softening his cruelty with any excuses. He added that, in fact, he did not know her at all and that he did not wish to go on encouraging, in spite of himself, the nonsense that she called love. Neither did he wish her to go on writing to him. The

refusal was categorical. Should he receive any
further letters from her he would send them back
without opening them. The conversation was
very short. He refused to listen to her protestations and laments. And should she phone him
again he intended to hang up. He had closed all
the doors on her. He had taken away the only
firm ground on which she walked. The strange
substitute form of existence that writing was for
her had been entirely destroyed. When she wrote
to him she existed for him. And it was only in
writing that her love found some expression.
What was left for her now if he refused to read
her letters? I felt guilty, thinking that Agustín
Valdés' sudden cruelty was the result of my inter-
ference. I did not know which was worse for Elsa,
the desolation of her solitary love or the overwhelming void into which Agustín had cast her.

The next day, impelled perhaps by the need to
deny the agonizing end that he had imposed on
her, she sent another mesage to Agustín Valdés.
It was a reproduction of a Goya print, a man
leaning over a woman whose face was half concealed by a mask. He seemed intent on guessing
her identity. Underneath were written the words:
'No one knows himself.' It hung on a wall in her

house. She took it out of its frame and putting it in an envelope posted it in the letter box. After that she drifted for several hours along mountain paths, through the streets of the village, up and down the stairs and through the rooms of her house. . . . Finally she set out to find the postman and begged him to give her back her letter. I don't know what reasons she gave, but she succeeded in getting it back. She kept the reproduction amongst the other objects already forming part of her love story.

For a few days I heard nothing of her. I hoped she would visit me, but she didn't. I was no longer in the habit of going down to her house for I always met Matilde there, purposely putting herself up as a barrier between Elsa and me, prohibiting any conversation between the two of us. Without any doubt she held me responsible for the state into which Elsa had fallen. She even got round to saying that from the very beginning she had considered that my hypnotic experiments were extremely dangerous. And as things stood, according to her, I represented an obstacle to any sort of help Elsa might get, assuming, that is, it was still possible to change her fate. Matilde doubted it, seeming convinced of Elsa's inevitable perdition. But in any event, she had decided to look after her while she needed it.

At last I went to visit her one evening. Matilde opened the door.

'Elsa's asleep,' she informed me drily, using the same tone of voice I had used to address that very sentence to her some time before.

She immediately invited me to sit down with her in front of the fire. Who knows whether she did it in the secret hope that I would refuse and leave her alone? I accepted, hoping she would give me some information about what was happening, for it occurred to me that it was too early for Elsa to be asleep.

'She sleeps a lot just now,' she explained without my asking anything.

We both stayed silent. I hoped she would decide to tell me a little more, seeing that she had established herself as Elsa's Cerberus. But Matilde calmly rocked back and forth in her chair, pretending to be unaware of my presence. I don't know how long I remained beside her, putting up with her uncomfortable silence and hoping that Elsa would appear at any moment. It seemed to me that the house had acquired an alarming atmosphere, without my quite knowing to what it was due. Lights were on everywhere; it might even be said that there was too much light. But nevertheless, I perceived a deeper darkness that refused to be dispelled. It was a morbid, living darkness, brittle, almost vibrating in that oppressive silence. Matilde rose to go to the kitchen. She was preparing supper for Elsa. She considered her so ill, she declared, that if nobody looked after her she would die. I suggested calling the doctor.

'Him! He doesn't know anything,' she answered, 'and what's more he never visits anyone further down than the church. He's too fat to walk up hills. The matter with Elsa is that she doesn't want to live. The birds she had in her head have left her.' I didn't answer. To a certain extent, what she said was true. Yes. What other illness could she have?

Matilde's slight person glided untroubled through that atmosphere, in harmony with it, watching me from it with her intense eyes. She wanted me to leave. I felt it intuitively even though she did not let it show, either in her words or in her attitude towards me.

'Why is it that Elsa sleeps so much?' I asked, really worried.

She answered that the nights were very long
for her. At times she heard her call in her sleep.
And whether she slept or not, the hours of darkness no longer brought any repose. In fact, quite
the reverse; during the day she felt quieter and
slept better. She added that she herself had
decided to spend the nights here, in this house, at
least until Elsa got better.

The next day I called at my friend's house
earlier, straight after school. It was still afternoon and I hoped that Matilde wasn't going to
remain there, shut up with her, at all hours of the
day and night. The door of the patio was open, as
also that of the sitting room. I went in without
knocking and found Matilde in the kitchen preparing herb tea with plants with strong sedative
properties; she had picked them herself and was
mixing them according to an old recipe.

'She needs to rest and not think about anything,' she said when she saw me.

'But if she's not asleep now, I'd like to see her.'
It irritated me to find myself asking the permis-
sion of this old woman to see my friend.

'It's better you don't see her.'

'What do you mean?'

'That I won't be able to do anything if you see

her,' she said, making it quite clear that she did not propose to give me any further explanation.

I understood that she now saw in me an obstacle that would prevent her gift of healing from doing any good to Elsa. As Matilde crossed the room to guard the door to Elsa's bedroom, I felt a strong desire to run there first, pushing her violently out of the way. But I didn't do anything. It was quite evident that Elsa needed to rest and forget. I left, resigned to not seeing her for some time, and with the same resignation, returned next day. Night had fallen when I pushed open the door and I was surprised at not meeting the old watchdog immediately. From the doorway I could hear a murmur of voices and a tinkling of glass. I approached the bedroom quietly – I was afraid Matilde would emerge silently from some door or corner and bar my passage. I reached it at last and stopped, framed in the doorway, visibly eavesdropping. I didn't even greet them. Matilde was busy singing the praises of the ferruginous water she had had someone bring from a medicinal spring and did not notice my presence. Elsa, with an exaggerated expression of disgust on her face, was handing back to Matilde a champagne glass still full of reddish water, mineral and disgusting. Matilde poured the contents of the glass back into the same bottle from which she had taken it. Then she noticed me observing her, but without saying a word, started tidying up Elsa's clothes. Her figure seemed to expand, to extend beyond its own limits, as she moved about the room, as though she would fill the whole space with her rhythmical coming and going. Elsa greeted me with a gesture of relief and pleasure. She was openly good-tempered and grateful to her nurse, but at the same time she already seemed tired of her constant presence.

'How do you feel?' I asked.

'I'm all right,' she answered. 'I'm going to get up this very moment. I've already spent several days drowsing, and anyway I don't want to give Matilde any more trouble.'

Her voice sounded artificially cheerful. Matilde sat on a chair at the foot of the bed and glowered at me fiercely. Elsa sat up with a certain effort; she was already dressed and suggested we go for a walk. I thought she wanted to get away for a while from the vigilance to which she had been subjected.

Bathed in moonlight, my friend's face was that of a wax figure. I sensed in it something not human, something not real. She walked beside me, heedless of where we were going. Thanks to my questions I found out that she spent her time collapsed on her bed, lost in a vacant time without pictures or words, plunged in a drowsy state that was always the same. It wasn't boredom, she said, but something else. It was the defenceless contemplation of an emotion, unique and intense, which could not now survive without outside stimulus, which was falling apart and losing its identity, but would not disappear. She told me also that she had decided to leave. She didn't yet know where she would go, but she wanted to leave the house she was in, which seemed to her to be riddled with holes. Holes everywhere, vertical, horizontal, upstairs and downstairs, in every corner and stairway. She felt faint as she went past each door. She didn't know what she feared: hands without body? Cats? Ghosts? Genuine intruders? She didn't know, but the house held her captive and paralysed. Matilde's presence, tedious though it might seem, had allowed her some peace, and, thanks to her care, she had been able to rest, something she had not been able to do for a long time.

While she talked, slowly, pausing for breath, I

noticed how transformed she was. She looked like a doll now, like something unreal. As she walked, her arms hung motionless and rigid close to her body. She had taken on the appearance of a very old woman whose every movement was a fight against stiff joints. We walked for more than an hour. I became tired of wandering up and down the streets of the village and suggested going to my house, to which she agreed. She didn't care whether she was standing up or sitting down, in the street or in a house. Nothing mattered to her, neither cold nor sleep, nor weariness nor the time of day . . . nothing. Her lack of interest in life infuriated me and I searched impatiently for some words to wake her up.

'Where do you think of going?' was all I could manage.

'I don't know,' she answered, 'I'd like to get away from everywhere. For ever.'

Her words struck me, of course, as an allusion to suicide. I tried to answer her constructively but the word 'life' slipped from my mind as I tried to evoke it.

'It's cowardly to commit suicide.'

I don't know how I could have uttered such an inanity. She looked at me disconcerted and I felt

ridiculous. In fact I hadn't offended her, at the
most I might have disappointed her.

I chose to keep quiet. The only words that
came to my mind were common-sense platitudes, or tactless remarks that could in no way
help her but were closest to my actual thoughts.
Elsa, sitting beside me in front of the fire as she
had so often done before, was sunk in an alarming immobility, as though everything that surrounded her had paused in solidarity with her.
Her eyes lacked the slightest spark of life and her
face, suddenly grown old, seemed to me that of a
stranger.

17

I went to fetch Elsa before dawn. I had promised to go with her to the bus and help carry her luggage up the steep hill that led from her house. We arrived at the top much too early and took our breakfast together in the bar, eating slowly as morning appeared through the window panes with a cold, ashen light. She would be in Granada at noon and would take a night train to Madrid where she had lived for the last few years. She now had no alternative, she said, but to return there and work, teaching if possible, for that was the only thing she knew how to do. Her parents had died some time ago. An aunt, her mother's sister, occasionally sent her a little money, but it was not enough to allow her to live in town. She was not in the habit of talking about such things and when she did it was in passing, a hurried interruption to be passed over quickly so as to get on with the other conversation, the one that mattered, the important one. While we waited, she imagined out loud her life in the future, wandering round the city, seeking past friends, taking up old projects already doomed, always departing, always abandoning whatever she encountered. She refused to envisage the possibility of any change, of any renewal of her life. Her past years seemed to her now – from up here – fragmented, broken, scattered over a ruined field whose sole survivor was Agustín Valdés, untouchable by time, the force which runs through everything that exists and leads inevitably to destruction. Her love had resisted the disintegration that threatened it. She remembered Agustín Valdés intensely, as though he really had been a close and tender friend.

'I'm not leaving!' she said suddenly, with relief. 'I can't. I'm too tired. I'm staying here. I don't know for how long.'

Her sudden decision disconcerted me. Last night, when she had confirmed that she was leaving, I had felt the silence anew, more intense, really disturbing. I thought about myself, my life, the void her absence would leave. I had lived so immersed in the story of her love, a story apparently external to me, that at no time had I realized how deeply I had become involved. But in spite of that, I said:

'You must go. You've got to get back to your normal life and do something.'

'My life can be anywhere, and what's more, I haven't got anything to do,' she answered.

I speculated that among other reasons she might have given for refusing to go to the city was a reluctance to leave these mountains. For us, up here, life seemed to halt, and linger so that we could rest, escape and play. Nothing seemed really essential up here.

Elsa stayed on, but I felt her absence as much as if she had left the village. She avoided us, both Matilde and me. She insisted on staying alone in the house, and walking endlessly in the mountains. Sometimes, when I saw her, she seemed absolutely transparent, as though nobody now inhabited her. She never mentioned Agustín Valdés again. Not once did she allude to her love nor to that strange story, which now, and for ever, would remain only half disinterred.

In spite of her unsociable and aloof attitude, I went to visit her several times running, but never managed to see her. The doors of her house were always open and the lights turned off. I knew that she came back from her walks very late. She had told me herself that she used to climb up to very distant places, near the Veleta peak where the mountains are snow-covered nearly all year round. She said that up there the silence of the snow was more intense than any thought or emotion could be; that immersing oneself in that immobility was like leaving the boundaries of one's body and becoming stillness, whiteness and silence. She assured me that in that timeless whiteness she had, at last, found something resembling peace.

One day I went to see her very early in the morning, before going to school, in the hope of finding her asleep. The door of her house was still open and there was nobody inside. I was appalled at the idea that she might have spent the night out of doors. In the period leading up to that morning, Matilde too had been upset and alarmed, to the point of nearly reconciling herself with me. She had insisted on continuing with her frustrated attempts at curing Elsa. Despite the fact that I knew she was genuinely fond of Elsa, I suspected that her perseverance was also aimed at protecting the reputation of that supposed gift of hers, which currently was systematically letting her down. During those days all Matilde could do was wait for Elsa, seated at the entrance to her house, remaining on watch during the hours of sunlight. Then, when the last rays disappeared behind the Tajo Gallego, she would immediately rise and return to her own house. Nowadays she seemed to attribute an obscure meaning to the nights and never visited Elsa after sunset. Alarmed that morning by Elsa's absence, I decided to go out and look for her. I cancelled school and drove my car towards the snow-covered peaks until the track, concealed by snow, became impassable. I continued on foot, calling out my friend's name in that indescribable solitude. I wandered about, recognizing many places that she had spoken of. At last, on an expanse of immaculate snow, I found her body, her dark hair, her crystallized face. She was rigid, motionless, clinging to the ground, become one with the mountains, the plants, the trees, the rocks and stones, all of them equally covered with the whiteness of snow. From the highest summits, from the Mulhacén and the Veleta, frozen and inhuman peaks, a bitter wind blew down and whipped my body. That grandiose and frozen scene took hold of me. I could do nothing. I could not think. At last, I let myself fall next to Elsa, overcome by the mighty silence of the mountains

and of death. It seemed to me that she vibrated
now with the pulse of the earth. I wanted to leave
her there for ever, in that element which she herself had chosen, so distant from the world of
men, leave her to fuse with it, to be owned by it,
as though she had at last found the place where
she belonged. There, time ran differently,
became other, immense, quiet, endless. For a few
brief moments her death filled me with deep
peace. But suddenly I was afraid. A dreadful cold
was immobilizing my jaws, my hands, my legs. I
ran to fetch my car and brought it as near as I
could. Painfully, I picked up Elsa's stiff body,
fighting against the slowness of my movements,
and placed it half-leaning on the back seat. Doing
this took me a long time; or perhaps it was a
different, strange time I was experiencing that
did not move, that never passed. I fled from that
awesome place which had received Elsa, wrapping her in its inhuman peace. I don't remember
thinking of anything as I drove. When I reached
the village I asked help of various black-clad
women who approached us fearfully and observed us curiously. Then, perhaps moved by a
sudden surge of hope, I asked them to fetch the
doctor. They helped me carry Elsa's body down

to her house. We stretched her on her bed and the doctor arrived shortly after. They had told him that she was dead, or at least appeared to be. Nonetheless, he examined her, wondered, tried to listen to her heartbeats, kept silence a few moments, and finally announced that she had died more than twenty-four hours ago. Matilde covered her body with a white sheet, and with some of the other women, stayed beside her, sitting on a chair prepared to watch over her till the hour of her burial. And then, as though she felt she had not been able to do anything for her in life, as though she were in debt to her, she insisted on offering her a present now that she was dead. She gave her her niche. Thus Elsa would receive the rays of the sun all day. A flash of mistrust made me suspect that Matilde wanted to get rid of it, that she preferred to start again on the long path of saving up enough money to buy herself another, giving her the illusion, perhaps, that she was postponing her appointment with death. I wanted to protest, but didn't dare forbid her gesture. And anyway, I felt now that nothing mattered. But imagining Elsa enclosed in that neat hole, the property of Matilde, suddenly made her death real and horrible. Faced with those sinister symbols: coffin, niche, cemetery, I succumbed to an overpowering anguish, at last fully realizing the definite disappearance of my friend. I bitterly regretted not having left her up there, amidst the snow-clad summits, in that beautiful tomb that she herself had chosen.

In the familiar sitting room, close to the hearth, now full of cold ash instead of fire, I found some objects that Elsa had left for me. She had arranged them on a small wooden table covered with a velvet cloth. There was the blue dried flower that she called 'love-in-a-mist', a postcard reproduction of a painting by Paolo Uccello, *Saint George and the Dragon*; an old Chinese box, and other things that had been part of her love story and prompted her immoderate feelings. She also left a letter addressed to Agustín Valdés, which she had not sealed. I could not help reading it. All she sent him was a short story by Kafka, *The Silence of the Sirens*, copied out in her hand. She had underlined certain passages:

'Ulysses, who thought only of wax and chains. . ..'
'Had they been aware of it the sirens would have been destroyed that day. . ..'

I sealed the envelope and sent it off without adding anything. I feared that Elsa's death would not affect him now as it had in her dreams, dreams in which she had loved him so intensely.

Capileira 1979–80
and May–June of 1985

Flamingo

Flamingo is a quality imprint publishing both fiction and non-fiction. Below are some recent titles.

Fiction
- [ ] Home Thoughts *Tim Parks* £3.95
- [ ] Human Voices *Penelope Fitzgerald* £3.95
- [ ] Offshore *Penelope Fitzgerald* £3.95
- [ ] Nelly's Version *Eva Figes* £3.95
- [ ] The Joys of Motherhood *Buchi Emecheta* £3.95
- [ ] The Thirteenth House *Adam Zameenzad* £3.95
- [ ] My Friend Matt and Hena the Whore *Adam Zameenzad* £3.95
- [ ] Night Night *Sharman Macdonald* £3.95

Non-fiction
- [ ] The Dancing Wu Li Masters *Gary Zukav* £4.95
- [ ] The Book of Five Rings *Miyamoto Musashi* £3.95
- [ ] Home Life *Alice Thomas Ellis* £3.95
- [ ] More Home Life *Alice Thomas Ellis* £3.95
- [ ] In the Ditch *Buchi Emecheta* £3.95
- [ ] Uncommon Wisdom *Fritjof Capra* £4.95
- [ ] The Turning Point *Fritjof Capra* £3.50
- [ ] The Tao of Physics *Fritjof Capra* £3.50
- [ ] Feeding the Rat *Al Alvarez* £3.95

You can buy Flamingo paperbacks at your local bookshop or newsagent. Or you can order them from Fontana Paperbacks, Cash Sales Department, Box 29, Douglas, Isle of Man. Please send a cheque, postal or money order (not currency) worth the purchase price plus 22p per book (or plus 22p per book if outside the UK).

NAME (Block letters) _____

ADDRESS_____

_____

_____